I NEVER READ THOREAU

A MYSTERY NOVEL BY KAREN SAUM

NEW VICTORIA PUBLISHERS

Published by New Victoria Publishers Inc., a feminist, literary, and cultural organization, PO Box 27, Norwich, VT 05055-0027.
Cover Art by Claudia McKay

1   2   3   4   5   6   2000   1999   1998   1997   1996   1995

Library of Congress Cataloging-in-Publication Data

Saum, Karen, 1935-
    I never read Thoreau : a mystery novel / by Karen Saum.
        p.   cm.
    ISBN 0-934678-76-6 (pbk.)
    I. Title.
    PS3569. A7887I5   1996
    813' .54--dc20   96-19899
                                                  CIP

Printed in Canada

For Peter, Lawrence and Stephen Reichard, three good men, my sons, from whom I have learned many important things about love and nurturing, friendship and loyalty.

PROLOGUE

In 1987, Brigid Donovan, a former nun turned amateur sleuth, became involved in the disappearance of one Chester Brown, aka Carlos Pardo, an agent of the Immigration and Naturalization Service of the United States Government. Details of that mystery and how she solved it are to be found in her account of the affair, *Murder is Germane*.

I Never Read Thoreau is a record of the same incident from the perspective of another player in the drama, Alexandra (Alex) Adler, former history professor and, at the time the events took place, a Jill-of-all-trades in Maine.

Adler's perspective is that of an insider and throws a somewhat different light on the matter, including a not very flattering portrait of Brigid Donovan, who makes what one might call a cameo appearance.

Those readers familiar with Donovan's rather head-long involvement in the mysteries that seem to inform her life—some say confuse her life—will not be prepared for Adler's more laid-back meandering approach. But the circumstances under which the bulk of the present account were written led Adler to tell many incidental stories, amusing in themselves, though not, perhaps, directly related to the solution of the mystery which prompted her to write in the first place. If the reader has never lived through a three-day Northeaster, or if she has difficulty imagining someone could write a memoir in one sitting, perhaps that reader should wait until a Northeaster strikes to begin this story.

CHAPTER ONE—BROWN

Brown, brown, feeling down, heart's so low it's underground.

Let's see. My name is Alex Adler, and in case this turns out to be my last testament, I guess I should make it my will, too. I want my tools to go to Scott, and if he doesn't want them, I guess Santa Clara might as well have them. And if anyone wants my car, they're welcome to it. If they decide to cremate me, I'd like my ashes put on Ellie Goldberg's compost pile because her flowers are seriously beautiful. Probably she wouldn't want me except I was ashes already.

I forgot to mention; there's a body here with me. God, I hope I don't join him. As a corpse I mean.

Hold on, Alex, steady as she goes. This is the plan...

No. First: This is the situation: I'm on an island called Monte Cassino. Alone. Well, except for the body. I found it at the foot of the stairs. Ladder really. I'm in Immaculate Conception. Where Sister Benedict lives now.

He must have slipped. His neck looks broken. I sort of rolled him in a quilt and got him on the sofa, out of the way. I probably shouldn't have moved him at all.

What happened io I heard on the scanner the police were going to raid the island, so I came on out. When I got here a dusting of snow had turned into a blizzard. I came across anyway. But the only person I found is what's-his-face.

Dead. It's snowing too hard to leave or I would. This blizzard's a Northeaster and it looks like it could go on forever.

If I don't survive, what I most want to say is I really don't know who this guy is and except for rolling him in the quilt and putting him on the sofa so I wouldn't trip over him—and wouldn't have to look at him—I've never had anything to do with him. Not really. I mean, it's true that I did work for him once. But I don't even know what his real name is, or why he used to spy on me, and I had absolutely nothing to do with his death. This is the truth. Really.

Okay. This is my plan. I've been here about three hours now and if anything it's snowing harder than ever. If I don't do something constructive I know I'm going to lose it. So, what I'm going to do is I'm going to start at the beginning and record the whole story.

I am writing on big sheets of newsprint using pastels and crayons. Sister Benedict is an artist. Thinks she is anyway. What I'll do is, instead of using one color until it's worn out, I'll use different colors to kind of give the emotional flavor of the story as I tell it. I have now just picked red, because Chester caught us 'red'-handed transporting refugees; this is an unpardonable pun, but he was a 'red' neck if ever there was one; and if I stay up all night writing, I'll be 'red'-eyed by morning.

Maybe I better go back to brown and start with what's-his-name. Chester Brown. Get him out of the way. In case something happens. Then I'll start at the beginning.

Actually, there's not much to say about Chester Brown. I don't even think that's his real name. Probably he was a government agent. Probably with Immigration and Naturalization. And probably the reason he harassed us all the time was because of how we brought the refugees from Central America and helped them get into Canada.

Or maybe, maybe, he was with the Drug Enforcement Agency. Tobacco and Fire Arms? I don't think so. My money's on the INS. I can think of several reasons why someone might want to kill him. But it looks like he just stumbled going up the ladder and broke his neck on the way down.

If I told Santa Clara once I told her a hundred times someday someone would break his neck on that ladder, and for once I was right. Probably.

To be completely honest—which I should because this really could turn out to be my last testament—Maria did say she was afraid Rollie might do in Chester Brown one day. But I don't see how that's possible. I didn't see anyone on the island and I checked every building after I came over.

Believe me, Rollie isn't someone you would overlook. He's about six-foot-ten and weighs a ton. I am positive that except for what's-his-face over there, there's no one on Monte Cassino but me.

Well, there isn't much more to tell about the body, about Chester Brown, if that's his name, so now I'll write about this island, Monte Cassino, and the people who founded the community here, Santa Clara and Sister Benedict. Where I am now, Immaculate Conception, is Sister Benedict's house. I once lived on this island, too. Lived here with Santa Clara. Now I live nearby, in Blue Hill, Maine. I used to think living here on Monte Cassino was the worst thing that could ever happen to me. I can see now, though, that I was wrong. Dying here would be worse. Oh, well. On with the story.

CHAPTER TWO—ORANGE

Oranges and lemons say the bells of St. Clements.

I used to call her Santa Clara. She'd protest, but her protests were always half-hearted: "Oh, Alex. Don't." I think secretly it pleased her, like everyone calling her Sister when she wasn't. Not any more. She'd joined young. Before Vatican II. I have a picture of her in coif and veil and black, long-skirted habit. Her eyes are turned, mournful, toward heaven, the way they are a lot in life. Now a bandanna frames her face, black with white, not unlike the coif and veil, both severe, both hiding the glory of her hair, which is red, a deep brick red, thick and curly as a horse tail, but soft to run your fingers through.

Her face, long-suffering and sweet, is like those martyred saints on the cards they used to give us at St. Anne's, trimmed in gold, each saint looking like all the others, but you know who it's supposed to be by the distinguishing sign: St. Theresa with her garland of roses, St. Catherine and her wheel. My Santa Clara has a mole beside her left eyebrow, near the center of her forehead which is, like her cheek-bones, broad, broad like her mother's people, Passamaquoddy from the reservation up to Perry.

Except for her hair, red as Georgia clay, Santa Clara looks Indian. Her eyes are brown, and her brows. Her brows are brown and thick and they cross her forehead in a line that's always straight and even, always serene. The mole's a different story, however. The mole is fed by a network of veins which, when she is angry, become engorged with blood and swell, the only perceptible sign that she's pissed, unless you count the fact that the angrier she gets the quieter she gets, so sometimes she goes around for days not saying a word to anyone. She calls it meditating.

Once, in the convent, she meditated so long at her Formation Director—she was protesting Vatican II with a water fast, wanting Mass to be said again in Latin—that the Formation Director finally directed her out of the order. When she left, she took Sister Benedict with her. Which was lucky. Or shrewd. Sister Benedict's family has megabucks. They used to own the half of Central America that Standard Fruit didn't. Sister Benedict's mother bought them the island off the coast of Maine that I'm on now and gave her blessing to a new order.

She also sent them Father Frank who, apparently, claimed to know Latin which, at best, was an exaggeration. Father Frank was a marathon runner, manqué, and seemed to feel that Mass cut into his morning run. His version of Mass, in English, took ten minutes. In Latin, more like fifteen. High holy days, and whenever Sister Benedict's family came to visit, he said Mass in Latin. Otherwise it was strictly English.

Santa Clara meditated at Father Frank a lot, but he never seemed to notice. I have a fantasy sometimes. My great, great, great, great granddaughter—this is like in the year 2200—will get one of those little cards trimmed in gold, for deportment maybe, or penmanship, and it will be a picture of Santa Clara. My Santa Clara. You'll be able to tell who it is because of the mole and the great angry veins feeding into it. Because someday someone's going to brain my Santa Clara for meditating at them once too often. That Cyclopean mole is what'll unhinge them. That mole will be her mark of martyrdom. Believe me.

Anyway, Santa Clara and Sister Benedict got this island, Monte Cassino, which is about a mile long by three-quarters of a mile wide. It's connected to the mainland by a sandbar you can drive on, but only for about five hours a day. There's a kind of bowl on the south side of the island, about ten acres of fairly flat land, and not too rocky. It opens onto a cobblestone beach facing east.

The community buildings, the barn, Trinity, the retreat houses, are protected by woods, mostly fir, growing on the island's granite rim, called Soper's Ridge. A stream runs through the pasture. It was in full spate when they first saw it, in April. Spring run-off. A cedar bog covers about fifteen acres on the island's western side.

That's where they built Immaculate Conception, the building I'm in now. Me and the body, aka Chester Brown (maybe).

In addition to the island and Father Frank, Sister Benedict's mother gave them her blessing, two-thousand dollars and the name of a dowser. The story goes Santa Clara wanted to spend the two-thousand dollars buying horses. Sister Benedict wanted to put in a well. Santa Clara argued a vision of the Blessed Virgin and employed meditation. Sister Benedict argued prudence and employed a well-driller. The story may be apocryphal. If it's true, Sister Benedict shot her bolt. She never defied Santa Clara again.

The dowser was worth her fee. The well came in at sixty feet though farmer Drinkwater's rig went down to a hundred before he could stop it. Still, there was enough money left over to buy a horse, a chainsaw and a bunch of nails.

Santa Clara discovered her métier felling trees. Which would have surprised anybody who knew her background— Boston-Irish. Her parents met one summer at Bar Harbor. Love at first sight. For the Boston-Irish youth, at least. For the young Passamaquoddy maiden, taken as an infant from her family and raised by whites, it may have been more like the prayed-for salvation from her racial limbo.

The trees that Santa Clara felled that summer, she and Sister Benedict milled on a portable bandsaw. The two of them lived in a tent and a lean-to while they constructed a log cabin about ten by twelve. Sister Benedict, of course, was even less accustomed to this mortification of the flesh than Santa Clara who, as the oldest child of an alcoholic father, had learned renunciation early.

Her father, during bouts of alcoholic remorse, had imposed, while she was growing up, fasts of expiation on all his family. From this it had been an easy step for little Clara to learn a method for becoming less vulnerable: control. And since she also learned to keep her distance emotionally, you might say what she learned was remote control.

In November, when Sister Benedict and Santa Clara moved into their little cabin, Santa Clara's new horse, Jonathan, inherited the lean-to for winter shelter. Father Frank commuted that first winter, running the sandbar when tide and ice permitted.

That winter Jonathan wasn't up for much work, but he flourished. Santa Clara got him for fifty dollars from a dying woodsman who, faced with the choice of buying a bottle of Thunderbird or grain, for the past several months had pretty regularly chosen Thunderbird.

Santa Clara had heard of their plight one day—she had been meditating at Sister Benedict while the well was being drilled—and she rowed over to investigate. That same evening, she led Jonathan by a rope halter back across the sandbar, having put a ten dollar deposit down on him. Ten dollars and a gallon of wine.

All this happened a long time ago—in 1970, when the whole world started going young and getting crazy. Take me for instance. In the '60s, if you remember back that far, everyone was serious, not to say responsible, me especially. Like, would you believe a college professor? A single parent?

(Remember, it's the '60s I'm speaking of, the decade following the '50s.)

And I'm not talking widow. I'm talking divorced woman. I'm talking four kids a year apart. I'm talking high heels and skirts never mind the weather. Responsible! My kids were responsible for integrating the schools in New York City. All of us were responsible for integrating the South, and that's not to mention ending the war in Vietnam. It's a good thing the Beatles came along when they did. They got us ready for the '70s.

As if in preparation, in '69 I lost my kids. Much later someone said to me, "How could you lose your kids?" She meant it sarcastically, a sure sign, though I didn't recognize it at the time, feminism was on the wane. I got mad and didn't tell her. But it was easy. This is how: They visited their dad the summer of '69, per divorce stipulation, but, unknown to me, he had arranged to remarry and move to another state where, of course, we had no custody agreement. (This is before the Uniform Custody Act, by the way. This method I'm describing of losing your kids wouldn't work any more.)

I managed to kidnap two of them back, but was foiled in my attempt for the other two. For me it was all or nothing, so I gave back the two I had. Later, after his next divorce, he tried to give all four of them to me again. But by then we were well into the '70s, and they were well into their teens and drugs, and what I said was, "Get lost!" I meant him.

We were camping on Mykonos that summer of '69, me, and the kids, and Maria Papandreou, my lover. Maria's husband at the time was a Greek policeman and we were camping in his backyard. Maria is a red-head from Harlem and a painter.

In hindsight you can see it was nearly the '70s. No one was supposed to be visiting Greece. The colonels were still in power. But there we were and Maria even married to a Greek, a policeman at that, worry beads, long pinky nail and all. But that's another story.

On the morning in question, we were supposed to be going to Delos for the day when who shows up at the tent flap but Clarence for the kids. This was a shock for several reasons. One being that since May his monthly letter contained nothing but a sheet of paper with this same sentence written on it: I'm not sending child support this month because I don't know where you are.

He had tickets for all of them to fly back to Wichita the very next day so we missed the trip to Delos. This was a Tuesday. What I didn't know was that on Saturday he was getting married again. In fact I didn't find out for four weeks, not until the first of September when they were supposed to come back and didn't.

I left the tents standing in Maria's husband's yard and the two of us flew home to find them. Clarence had moved to Charlotte, North Carolina. Mecklenburg County, home to the Klan (though, presently, also to be home of the Wilmington Seven, and once home to Robert Williams). I doubted they took kindly in Mecklenburg County to dykes. So, as soon as I hit town I bought me some protective cover, a cute little organdy and lace mini-skirted dress, a pair of heels, straw hat with grosgrain ribbon, and shades.

I cased all the schools looking for the kids. Jennifer and Scott both walked right past me and didn't bat an eye which told me one thing: my disguise worked. It should have told me something else: Less than a month and they'd both been Southernized. If they'd seen me in a get-up like that on the streets of Brooklyn, they'd have split a gut laughing.

After I didn't manage to kidnap all four of them, and the two I did have wanted to go home—it was ninety-eight in the shade and that rat Clarence had rented what the kids kept calling their villa and it had a pool in back—I went to see a lawyer who recommended I not fight it. "These children are bad-mouthing you. Someone is teaching them a word I am sure they have no idea what it means." The word was "lesbian" and they knew exactly what it meant, but I sensed this was no time to take up linguistics.

He went on. "Now a judge is not going to be very receptive to that kind of talk. Not receptive at all." He spelled out what he meant by "not receptive at all."

"Here in North Carolina that means an orphanage. Neither parent was what he would consider fit. He would put them in an orphanage. No question about that. Kids shouldn't bad mouth their mothers." He shook his head sadly. "Not like that."

He was right. They shouldn't. Not in Mecklenburg County, North Carolina, anyway. Leastways, not in 1969. So I took the two I had, Timothy and little Clarence, back to their villa and their swimming pool. Along the way we had a desultory conversation about a big CORE demo planned for Borough Hall on Columbus Day. Their lack-luster attention to topics other than swimming pools, new bicycles, new dogs and villas, theirs especially, convinced me I had a responsibility to rescue them, bad mouthing and orphanages notwithstanding.

That night, however, I had my run-in with the Mecklenburg County vice squad. You see, on the day we arrived in Charlotte, Maria and I had looked in the Classifieds for a place we could afford to stay while I organized the kidnaping. We settled on a little hotel a block and a half from the Greyhound Bus Station right off the main drag. The lobby contained quaint Southern-looking rocking chairs with elderly Southern-looking occupants.

We didn't notice it was integrated, and, naive, even if we had, it wouldn't have alarmed us any.

A little after one in the morning the night of my failed kidnap attempt, someone pounding on the door woke us. "Poh-leece! Open up!" We scrambled out of bed and started pulling on our pajamas. "Poh-leece! Open up!" I could hear men's voices outside sniggering and carrying on. I called down to the desk. "There's a bunch of men outside in the hall. They're trying to get in the room," I said. Trying to sound indignant, voice quavering.

"Yes, ma'm?"

"Well," I said. "They say they're police."

"Yes, ma'm?"

"Well... You mean they are?"

The pounding on the door intensified. "Poh-leece! Open up this door yawl hear?"

"Yes, ma'm," said the voice in my ear, then he hedged. "I mean to say, the poh-leece is here and they is upstairs. Could be they's at yoh door. Yes, ma'm."

At the door Maria was saying, "You don't sound like police to me."

The voice on the other side, bullying, assured her. "We poh-leece all right. Ma'm, you have three choices. The first is you can open this here door. The second is I can break it down. And then, I can just shoot it down. What'll it be, ma'm?"

She opened the door and five or six men walked in, sniggering and looking around, looking at us especially. Their leader checked in the closet and behind the shower curtain. No one looked under the bed. Maria said, she has a slight, unidentifiable accent, by-product of a varied life, "You don't act like police to me."

Their leader swaggered over to her. The sniggering stopped. Like dogs on a short leash, their ears twitched with attention. "Oh we don't," he said. "Now, where're you from poh-leece act so different?"

Defiant, Maria said, "New York. New York City."

"Oh," he said. He said, gentle, like a lover, "New York City." A pre-snigger rustle stirred the men. "New York City. Well, ma'm, when you get back to New York City, you tell the poh-leece up there they can come down here to Charlotte any old time and we'll teach them how to be real poh-leece." The snigger broke like a wave on the beach. Then, without anyone remembering to check under the bed, they left.

The next day it was in all the papers. *VICE SQUAD RAIDS*

HOTEL. Our names were listed. From out of town. Without actually saying so, it made us look like hookers from the Big Apple. Even I could see after that there wasn't much point fighting for custody in Charlotte.

Next day I did call the ACLU. The ACLU in Mecklenburg County was one man. Mr. Annum. He'd gone to Harvard. As it turned out, he was preparing a case against the vice squad right then. All the other plaintiffs were black, he told me. Would I, when it came to trial, come down to testify? Why not? It was still 1969 and still each person's responsibility to make the world a better place to leave our children. Seriously. If you can't remember that far back, that's the way we thought about things then.

Right before he hung up, Mr. Annum couldn't help himself. He said, "What were you girls doing staying in that hotel, anyway?" Goes to show you, Jesus knew where the action was when it came to righteousness. The one place in Charlotte that was integrated in 1969—black and white, old and young—and it was a whorehouse.

CHAPTER THREE—RED

Red. Red. What I'd rather be than dead.

I think I should've used red for the sixties. They were kind of a red decade. Plenty of time for brown or orange later!

It's midnight now. The weather's gotten worse. Wouldn't have thought it was possible. At the rate I'm burning it, there's only enough wood to last another five or six hours. I wish to God I hadn't been so impulsive, hadn't come out to the island when I heard on the scanner that the police were raiding it.

I was worried about Maria. She went out to the island in the afternoon, said she was going to help Santa Clara roof the barn. I didn't want her to go, and we sort of had a fight about it. So when I heard about them on the scanner raiding Monte Cassino, I wasn't only scared, I was contrite. Okay, and jealous.

But mostly I was afraid Chester Brown, my corpse over there, had something to do with the raid and frankly, I distrust that man. Distrusted him. He was creepy and he scared me. But when I got here, there was no one around. No one. Except Chester—if that's his name, which I seriously doubt—and he was dead. I'm sure it was an accident. Though when you have a ladder like that one up to the loft, I'm not sure you can call it an accident when someone breaks their neck

15

like he did.

By the time I got to the sandbar, it was dark, of course, but I had the old lady's flashlight—more on that later—and so I managed to cross—on the ice—the tide was already coming in and that made me anxious, of course, about where Maria was.

Meanwhile, she's probably safe and warm back home wondering where I am.

Hey! Slow down, Alex. Chill out. Get a grip.

Okay. Here's the situation now: About an hour ago I went out to use the john; the snow was so bad I tied myself to the back door so I wouldn't get lost.

And another thing—even right next to the stove, it's almost too cold to write. But I know I can't sleep, not with the body there, not worrying like I am about what happened to everyone. So, I'll just go on with my story. Back to Santa Clara and the little community she and Sister Benedict started on Monte Cassino.

In the spring, Santa Clara and Sister Benedict evicted Jonathan, put Father Frank into the ten-by-twelve shed and moved themselves back into the tent and lean-to. Then they began construction of Trinity which for the next several years was to be the main building in the community here. Trinity has a central room for Mass and meetings, and two other rooms, like wings, one for Father, and one for guests. The plan was Santa Clara's, a sort of cruciform: Father, Son, and Holy Spirit. They kept on calling it Trinity even after the transfiguration of the eighties, which is when I came.

Father Frank was the shortest marathon runner I ever saw and, even though he ran ten K a day, except on days when he ran farther, he was also the fattest, which is funny because he didn't eat that much. Not really. Everyone in the community is fat. I got fat when I lived here. And it isn't that we ate so much. It's more like we ate so badly.

Take the Black Fast. The Black Fast was Sister Benedict's

mother's idea. She'd read about it. Some order of nuns, Carmelites, I think, did it. All during winter, right up until Easter, everything you eat has to be black. You wouldn't believe how much chocolate syrup we managed to get through in a winter. And coffee. We always had a buzz on. Sheer weight is all that kept us earth-bound. It doesn't happen all at once, but gradually you can get fond of chocolate scrambled eggs and coffee. Chocolate cottage cheese and coffee. Santa Clara used to whip up a dish of chocolate instant mashed potatoes and coffee, but I never cared much for that. Winter months lunch always seemed unappetizing to me, but breakfasts and dinners, where it was so dark anyway and you didn't notice how all the food was black, I got used to them. Lots of chocolate spaghetti sauce on brown rice (we cheated a bit there), and lots of chocolate cake. But like I said, we did get fat.

I think Black Fasts ruined Fr. Franks' life. He had a picture in his room at Trinity. He had a few pictures, but in this particular one he's about twenty and he's just won a race for St. Francis Xavier. He's by himself, so he doesn't look so short, though the trophy in his arms seems enormous.

Everyone when they first see this picture says, "Oh, who's this?" I know I did. You could tell it annoyed him, especially if, as happened a lot, the person came back with something like, "You're kidding!" or, "No, I mean this one." In the picture, his hair's wavy and kind of long and he has a gorgeous little mustache.

He wasn't meant to be the priest. But when his older brother, Thomas McGrath, was killed in Nam, naturally he entered seminary. Before that he had been studying law. In seminary, besides theology and that sort of thing, he studied psychology. And he continued to run. When he left the community, in the early '80s, he had fallen in love, but what with being five by five and having this taste for chocolate spaghetti sauce on rice, it just wasn't in the cards he'd be anybody's Mr. Right.

He got a job teaching up to the University and once in a while, when I'm up to Orono, I see him out running. I suspect, looking at him, he still keeps that Black Fast.

When Trinity was finished in the fall and Frank established in it, Santa Clara and Sister Benedict went back to the shed and turned the lean-to over again to Jonathan. By this time they'd run up some bills in the neighborhood. They owed practically everyone. They owed for taxes, for nails, for renting the band saw off farmer Drinkwater's son. They owed for chainsaw oil, and gasoline. They owed on the grain for Jonathan and what they owed for chocolate syrup was dizzying.

Father Frank still got a stipend from his order, but where both Santa Clara and Sister Benedict were out of order, they had nothing coming in. Nothing other than the little gifts Sister Benedict's mother sent on feast days, but theirs wasn't exactly a medieval calendar, and the community was always short of cash. That's kind of how they got to know Beulah.

One Sunday afternoon in October, while Santa Clara was watching the Boston Patriots on a little black and white TV she had hooked up to a spare car battery, and Sister Benedict, who couldn't stand football—"So much violence!"— was reading the *Bangor Daily Weekender*, Sister Benedict saw the ad that probably changed their lives, though they could hardly have realized that at the time.

"Here's slab wood for sale, fitted, only twenty-five dollars a truck load. Delivered. I wonder if they'd bring it out here."

The Pats were behind 35 to 3, fourth quarter, so Santa Clara unriveted her attention. "Slab wood's no good," she observed.

"It's better'n what we got which is nothing."

That was true. What with all the house construction and then football season starting, Santa Clara hadn't seen to their winter firewood. "There's still lots of scraps," said Clara, meaning the sticks and shavings and the slabs from farmer Drinkwater's son's little band saw.

"Yeah, but it won't see us through the winter."

"We got by all right last winter."

"I don't call that all right. Cutting down a tree in the morning you're going to burn that night. All green. Besides, what if something happened to you?"

And that was an interesting point, because neither Father Frank nor Sister Benedict would touch a chainsaw, not that Santa Clara would have let them touch hers. Still, they could have gotten one of their own and used it.

Santa Clara turned the TV back on in time for locker room interviews and Sister Benedict, afraid Santa Clara might start meditating, said no more about it. But the next day, Santa Clara saddled Jonathan and the two of them went in search of Beulah and her twenty-five dollar slabwood.

Beulah and her two silver Percherons: The three of them are a matching set, alike in their coloring, their size, and in their ponderous strength. When I met her, Beulah was getting on to sixty and solid still as quarried granite. The skin of her face, wrinkled as a piece of crushed velvet, is the only thing about her that looks soft. Her trunk is thick, like a Sumi wrestler's, and her limbs massive; she's close on six-foot tall and I'm talking summer when she wears jellies and cut-offs and a halter that disappears in the outcroppings of her breasts.

Summer and winter she and her Percherons harvest wood for pulp for a local sawmill, and for firewood. She started when she was six, working with her pa, after her mother, who had been his helpmate in the woods as in everything, miscarried on the kitchen floor, right in front of Beulah and her younger brother and sister, and died right there in a puddle of blood and placenta. Beulah said she could still see the scene clear as if it happened yesterday.

"We lived off the road some. Didn't have nothing but the two hosses and Pa was in the woods. Didn't get home 'til late. Way past dark. That's how I started."

For Beulah this is a long speech. By 'how I started' she

meant she took over care of the kids and helped with yarding. "Pa told me 'git' first time I went in. Just follered behind. Good thing. Got kicked. Accident, mind. Laid him open here," she slaps her thigh, "cut so big;" she holds her index fingers ten inches or so apart. "See the bone."

Beulah talks best when she talks with her horses, but you have to be close and listen carefully to hear. Plus watch. Her side of it is little clicks she makes with her tongue, and gentle twitches of the reins held slack in those great hands of hers. The horses, they talk mostly with their ears. They have ears more expressive than lots of faces I know.

Once the kids were grown and her pa passed on, Beulah lived alone, just her and the horses. It had been like that for nearly ten years the day Santa Clara arrived on Jonathan. Poor Beulah. It was love at first sight. Of Santa Clara, not Jonathan. By then Jonathan, on his own or next to Father Frank, for instance, looked pretty good. Next to Beulah and her Percherons, however, he was puny.

No, it was Santa Clara Beulah fell in love with. At forty-five, for the first time, and she had it bad. What with felling trees, building houses, and, of course, the Black Fast, Santa Clara had developed into a strapping woman. Not in Beulah's class, but strapping. For twenty-five dollars, Beulah agreed to deliver slab to the island and to teach Santa Clara how to yard with Jonathan.

In no time Beulah made other arrangements as well: "Decent," she said of the island's stand of trees. Looking around her in the shallow grassy bowl, she admired Trinity extravagantly.

She said, "No hardwood to speak of."

Assessing the cedar swamp, she judged, "Plenty of posts. Shingles too, most likely."

And then she made her offer: "Two acres of stumpage for instruction?" confident it would be accepted.

Sister Benedict was aghast. "You're not having that woman out here, Clara, are you crazy?"

When Sister Benedict was eating properly she was what they call a willowy blonde. About five-foot-ten and a long drink of water. Hair honey colored and, until they shaved it in the convent, half way down her back. Features: perfect. She looked a lot like Ingrid Bergman as a matter of fact, only skinnier. Or she had been skinnier before she moved to the island. After Beulah, she got skinny again and stayed that way, didn't seem to matter how much chocolate syrup she made away with winters.

According to Father Frank, Sister Benedict carried on about Beulah for months. He couldn't say whether Santa Clara and Beulah carried on. They spent their days in the woods and always a lot of wood to show for it. "A lot of wood," he said. So he doubted there was anything to it. Santa Clara meditated against Sister Benedict all that winter right through the Black Fast and up to Easter, but made up for it talking to Beulah and to the Percherons. It got so Clara could even talk to Jonathan and Jonathan understood, so she said. Who knows. He seemed to go on doing just as he damned well pleased same as before. If Benedict communed with anyone, it was with nature, Father Frank was too busy running.

Sister Benedict's carrying on about Beulah was so interesting to Father Frank, the carrying on and the reason behind it—sheer jealousy—he finally gave it a name. He called it the Sister Benedict Syndrome. He named it after the third or fourth time it happened. The next person to get the syndrome was Beulah herself, though it hadn't been named yet. I, in my day, got it too. Matter of fact, I still have it, sort of. But that's a few years down the road. When I get to that part of my story I intend to use black.

CHAPTER FOUR—BLACK

This is a before-the-Sister-Benedict-Syndrome occasion for using black.

If it hadn't been for the Sister Benedict Syndrome, I wouldn't be sitting here now on this god-forsaken island during the storm of the century (millenium's more like it) writing all this down. But actually, it was more because of Maria I was jealous than because of Santa Clara. I really believe I'm over Santa Clara. Maria, though, she's a different story. I wouldn't even be in Maine except for Maria, let alone here on Monte Cassino.

One of Maria's former husbands, Danny Pendleton, is a guide in the Allagash. That's the far northern part of Maine and it's wilderness. Somehow he tracked her down to that whorehouse in Charlotte.

He claimed that Costa, the Greek husband in whose backyard we had left our tents, said to him, "Call the operator in Charlotte and ask her to start ringing the brothels," and that's what he did.

Danny said, "You sure weren't staying at the best one." But I don't believe his story for one minute. Danny's always telling stories for a laugh, Maine humor they call it, and it's made him the most popular guide in the business.

"I have a proposition for you, Maria," he said.

"No more, Danny, no more," she said.

"Maria, this is one you can't turn down. Alex and the kids will love it."

Alex. That's me.

Maria's eyes rolled around in her head.

The cook in Danny's camp had up and quit on him. Hunting season starting in just two weeks, he wanted us to come help out. Through November.

What he wanted was Maria to come help out. He spoke to her painter's heart. He reminded her of autumn colors. The quality of light in the air on a frosty November morning as you look across Moosehead Lake, at the light lying flat and silver on the surface of the water. Light, refracted from crystals of ice, making fields of little diamond chips, blue and red and silver, that appear to hover above the snow. Of all Maria's husbands, Danny Pendleton knew her best.

But what he didn't know was, as of that very moment, I, Alex, had no kids enrolled in PS 135 and, harbinger of 1970, was free of all responsibility. I could quit my job and I did.

Ten days later, Maria and I flew to Greenville. I will say this for him: Danny put a good face on it.

Danny's camp is a little past Chesuncook, where Thoreau used to hang out. It's suffered a better fate than Walden Pond. These days you go in on an ATV. Then we hoofed it.

He had three bunk houses and for eight weeks a steady stream of hunters occupied them. Maria cooked and painted. I hauled water from the lake, changed beds and washed dishes. I also went canoeing a lot until it got too cold.

About mid-November, Danny had another proposition for Maria. Maybe there were more, but this is the only one I heard about. The only one I heard about Danny making. She got lots of propositions from different hunters. Maria told me about several of those. She thought it was funny. One she didn't tell me about; I found out on my own.

The hunter in question was a big Swede named Maj Pederson. In English, her name would be May. By big, I mean tall. Maj was built like a pole. Both she and Maria. But where

Maria's hair is red, Maj's is blonde, and I mean everywhere.

One afternoon I came in early from canoeing; the wind had come up and I was freezing. It was about 2:30, Maria's time to paint, which is why I took to going out in the first place, to get out of her hair as she put it. At the time I took it as a figure of speech.

I walked in and there was Maj, bare-assed naked putting wood in the stove. Maria was in bed. "What the fuck!" I said.

Maj said, quick as a wink, "Henny Penny. Felicitous Fornication."

Maria, on the bed, started kicking her feet in the air and laughing. "Oh, Maj!" she gasped. "You kill me." Which is what I wanted to do. "I know. It's a Ducky Fucky!"

Maj turned and stuck her hand at me. "Maj," she said. "We've never been introduced. You're supposed to be out canoeing."

Maj is a poet from New York City. She changes her shrink more than some people change their bed sheets. Her latest one prescribed a dose of back-to-basics. Chesuncook, Danny's address, caught Maj's poetic imagination and she came. Back-to-basics with Maria might not have been what Maj's doctor had in mind, but Maj was delighted.

Danny's proposition was that Maria occupy the camp all winter while he journeyed to Australia to explore the Outback. When Maria announced she intended to return to New York with Maj, he offered this proposition to me.

As propositions go, this one was definitely turn-down-able. I said why not.

A winter at Chesuncook. And I never even read Thoreau.

Black's a good choice for my first winter in Maine. As I remember it, I lived on black strap molasses and Jack Daniels. Talk about a black fast!

Maria left with Maj mid-November promising to write. Hunting season ended November 24, but Danny stayed on another week. He said to save money.

His charter flight didn't leave Boston until December 2nd.

But I think he was worried I couldn't make it through the winter there alone. If so, it was a worry we shared. Inertia close to despair is what made me say I would stay. I had never been alone in my life before, getting pregnant and married during senior year at college. And I'd never lived anywhere but in a city. Camping, for the sixties, had been first class, family tents and camper busses. This camp of Danny's past Chesuncook hadn't a hint of civilization in it.

Before he left, Danny fussed a lot. Every morning he split more of the wood stacked in a low wall between the kitchen door and the out-house. A skim of ice already covered the lake.

"Alex, listen, this is real important." He said this about eighty times a day. He said it especially about breaking the ice on the lake. "Keep the hole open and keep it as wide as you can. Also, don't forget to cover it with this." 'This' was an insulated cover about four feet across. "Otherwise in twenty-four hours you could get three, four inches of ice you're never goin' to break through. That means no water. And don't even think about trying to get by melting snow."

He maintained the snowmobile daily and tried to teach me how to. He gave me walking instructions on snow shoes and skiis. He fussed about the food stores, the bottled gas, the kerosene for lamps. He showed me at least a hundred times how to drill a hole to ice fish and how to set the signal.

"You're gonna get sick and tired of Spam and beans," he assured me. "So you're gonna wanta fish."

Before he left, he helped me close off the kitchen in the main camp where I'd be staying. Together we covered the windows with plastic, puttied the cracks, and banked the sides.

Chesuncook itself was two miles away. "You should drive over there regular on the snowmobile," he advised. "Otherwise, how you're inexperienced and all, you could lose your way real easy." And that would remind him to get out the compass and test me on how to use it. "Ain't no way in hell you gonna get outta here once them snow's startin' you don't know how to use this compass."

Then there was the medicine supply: a case of Jack Daniels, a case of Canadian Rye, and more beer than you could shake a stick at.

"But don't get drunk," Danny said, "until you get your water in for the day. In fact, best not to get drunk at all. Fire, you know. It's dangerous. Can be real dangerous." Then he would tell me some story about a camp and a camper who had come to a nasty, alcoholic end, bleeding to death or burning. His stories always made me thirsty.

That first winter in Maine at Chesuncook was the first winter for Santa Clara, Sister Benedict and Jonathan on their little island. Santa Clara has often told me that mine was the easier one. I try not to get into it on the general ground you shouldn't compare oppression.

Old timers say the year before there'd been more snow. Who cares. After snow buried the cabin, right past the windows, right past the eaves, so I had to tunnel to the lake for my water, the snow banks too high to fling a shovelful of new snow on top of the old, in short, after the first of January, who was keeping track?

My last trip to Chesuncook was on Christmas Eve. A bunch of nuns and volunteers from the *Catholic Worker* were there on retreat. I drank too much and they insisted I stay the night. Early next morning, Jimmy, a son of the family who took care of the place, rode over to replenish my fire and haul water. When the snow got to be more than I could handle, Jimmy began coming by to check up on me. Once in a while he'd bring someone with him, someone staying there at Chesuncook on retreat. That's how I met Jaspers.

My first conversation with Jaspers went something like this. We were sitting around the wood stove, Jaspers and me with a glass of Jack Daniels, Jimmy and Sister Marie Therese with a mug of hot chocolate.

"Adler," said Jaspers. That's my name, Alexandra Adler.

My mother was a great romantic. "Interesting name, Adler. No relation to Victor Adler I suppose." He laughed, winked and sipped his drink.

I said no. My dad, when he was a boy, lived in a town outside Belgrade, Futag. Ages ago, when it was still part of the Austro-Hungarian Empire. He spent his student days in Vienna,

"You know the name?" Jaspers asked.

Jaspers is an indeterminate age somewhere past forty. He reminds you of a crane, long, awkward, knobby. He either winks a lot or he has a slow tic, and when he gets excited about what he's saying, which is most of the time, he crosses his legs and jerks the top one back and forth.

"The Austrian Social Democrat?" I said.

"He was a friend of my mother's." Jaspers licked his upper lip, winked and jerked his leg around. I wondered did he mean to suggest he was Victor Adler's son? I tried to remember when Adler died. Decided, not knowing Jaspers' age, that it might be possible.

But it wasn't Adler that Jaspers wanted to talk about. It was his mother.

"She was a Russian Jewess. Sephardic. Her people came from Spain in the twelfth century. A friend of Kollontai." He cackled, his foot spinning in tight little circles. "You ever hear of Alexandra Kollontai, Sister?" he asked.

Sister Marie Therese kept her head buried in her mug of hot chocolate. Jimmy, looking ornery, said, "Yeah. She's my sister's best friend at school."

Jaspers ignored him and looked at me inquiringly. I nodded. "Yeah."

"Well, you know she and Lenin used to fight it out on the question of free love."

Sister Marie Therese put down her mug and took out her rosary.

"One day Kollontai said to Lenin, 'Love is necessary, like air, like water. Air is free. Water is free. Love must be free.'

27

"Lenin looked at her and he said, 'Yes, it is true, water is free. But we don't all use the same cup.'"

Jaspers started in laughing and licking his lips, his foot twitching, like a mechanical dog wound up too tight. Sister Marie Therese began to look more alarmed than scandalized. She said she thought it was time they left. Jaspers said he had another story to tell about his mother, about when she accompanied Trotsky to Mexico where he, Jaspers, was born.

"Another time, Jaspers," said Sister Marie Therese with surprising firmness. "Another time. It's starting to snow again."

I didn't see Jaspers after that until he showed up here on Santa Clara's little island some fifteen years later. Noticing the wide, flat planes of Santa Clara's face and her straight, brown brows, Jaspers revealed another lineage. "My mother's great, great, great, great grandmother was Pocohontas," he said and he licked his upper lip.

The little community on Monte Cassino didn't really start to grow until after the war in Vietnam wound down. I wonder sometimes if there'd been demos to go to, or even something like full employment, whether this little community would have flourished. Flourish it did, however, and housing people got to be a problem. Not a problem for Santa Clara. She was always happiest knocking down trees and building up houses. The problem was the planning board. They regarded Santa Clara's labors not so much God's work as sub-division. According to the planning board, you could build only twice every five years. For Santa Clara, that was like saying you could eat only twice every five years, and was out of the question. Like any good saint, she was tickled to defy authority. Sister Benedict was willing to go along with her, but within reason. Santa Clara wanted to call her fourth retreat house Holy Cross. Sister Benedict counseled caution: "If we call it the Tool Shed," she reasoned, "they'll never make us tear it down." And the Tool Shed it became.

Santa Clara prevailed in most things, but not when it

came to names. For instance, the name of the community itself. Santa Clara called it Rerum Novarum, but, unless you had "the day after" in mind, there wasn't much about the place you could call new, there being no electricity and no running water, just a few shacks and some out-houses.

After the lean-too, one shed, and Trinity, Santa Clara built three small retreat houses: St. Mary, St. Anne and St. Elizabeth. Her original intention had been to dig an out-house for each one also. But what with having to supply wood for five stoves, she ended by digging just one big hole for a two-seater, and she never got around to roofing it. That's when Father Frank rashly dubbed the place Gethsemane. He said whenever he used the out-house and it was twenty below or raining, he would find himself saying, "Let this cup be taken from me." Santa Clara was not amused.

It was the name Sister Benedict's mother gave to the island that finally stuck. She had called it Monte Cassino from the very beginning. This is how Santa Clara gave in and finally came around to accepting that name.

The winter of '70, according to Sister Benedict, there were four people living out on the island: Sister Benedict, Father Frank, Santa Clara and Beulah. Talk with Beulah, though, and you get the idea that during this Anno Domini of her life, Santa Clara and Jonathan lived out with her and her Percherons.

Whatever, the next summer, two Sisters of the Atonement and a Franciscan Brother moved to the island.

The Sisters of the Atonement were named Barbara and Michael. Coming together, they decided to stay together, at least at first. They used St. Mary to store their belongings and, apparently, they slept together in the loft of St. Anne. Either that or they took turns sleeping. The loft is only three feet wide. The Franciscan Brother, Andrew, resided in St. Elizabeth. He was of a scholarly bent and didn't stay long. He tried to engage Fr. Frank in theological disputations, but to no avail. Brother Andrew never went anywhere without an open book in his hand, so he was unable to jog with Fr. Frank, even if Fr. Frank had issued an invitation, which he never did. In fact, out walking one Sunday afternoon, his nose buried in the *Song of Songs*, Brother Andrew tumbled off the cliff and broke his leg like the pitcher broken at the cistern. He went away while it mended, and he never came back again.

Before the trees lost their leaves in October, Santa Clara had one of the new Sisters, Sister Barbara, using a chainsaw with her in the woods. It was a cute little red chainsaw about half the size of Clara's own. Barbara used it to four-foot and limb while Santa Clara strode around selectively felling trees the Extension Service had identified with strips of orange plastic tape. Beulah didn't approve at all. Through October she would come across the sand spit weekends with the Percherons. She'd stand there in her black and red plaid wool shirt and jeans, her steel-toed boots and hunter's cap, holding the reins slack in her hands, and she'd remonstrate softly to Santa Clara. "You don't need her," she'd say. "Sneeze and you'd blow her away. You and me, we can do all the logging you need, same as last year."

Santa Clara wouldn't say much, just press the trigger of her chainsaw so Beulah's voice got lost in the angry buzz of it, and red oil splattered around on the early morning snow like blood. Then Santa Clara took to knocking on the door of St. Anne before dawn and she and Sister Barbara would be off somewhere in the woods when Beulah came. All Beulah would get of Santa Clara was the sound of her chainsaw, hers and Sister Barbara's, like a duet, buzzing to each other far off in the woods.

There was no one for Beulah to talk to those days. Sister Benedict, whatever she might have felt about Sister Barbara, was relentlessly resentful of Beulah. When Fr. Frank wasn't running, he tended to be asleep, especially in winter. Brother Andrew did ask her views once on the historicity of Jesus.

She told him mildly that she had always disliked history and she couldn't abide cities. After that, Brother Andrew, if he ever happened to walk past her as she stood patiently outside Trinity hoping to see Santa Clara, never even bothered to raise his eyes from his book to greet her.

At first Sister Michael sensed a potential ally in Beulah to help break up the intimacy between Sister Barbara and Santa Clara. But Beulah was content just to wait and to hope, and wait she did until the heavy snows of winter came. Sister Michael about Christmas-time discovered a way to sublimate her passion in writing. Her first novel, a kind of Gothic Romance, ended up eight weeks on the Best Seller list. She ended up in California writing scripts for Hollywood.

Sister Michael's first novel was the inspiration for a pilot series on TV featuring some mildly scandalous intrigues among a group of nurses on an island in the English Channel. They were nurses British-style and so looked mighty like some Nuns. And of course, they were called Sister. The name of the pilot, and the island, was *Rerum Novarum.*

Santa Clara watched the first installment on her little black and white TV. Next day she said to Sister Benedict did she think Beulah would want to live at Monte Cassino with them. Sister Benedict is said to have burst into tears and gone into a long meditation against Santa Clara that lasted one whole week. Who knows. Beulah did not move to the island, though she continues to visit to this day. Sister Benedict's mother, when she heard of Santa Clara's capitulation in the matter of a name, forked over one hundred big ones to build a chapel on the island. She wanted them to name the chapel St. Benedict's.

And St. Benedict's it was. In the matter of names, Santa Clara had learned to accept defeat. But what she used the building for was a barn. When I first moved to Monte Cassino, she and I lived in part of it.

CHAPTER FIVE—BLUE

True blue NOT, but as in denim, blue.

Now I've explained a little about myself and about Monte Cassino you can see how strange it was not to find anyone here last night when I got to the island. Just that corpse over there. Chester Brown. If that's really his name, which I have reason to doubt.

What first struck me odd, there were no police running around. On the scanner it said they were raiding the place. And no one else was here either. There should have been a lot of people: refugees and volunteers, not to mention Maria and Santa Clara, and Sister Benedict.

But say I got here too late and everyone had been arrested already and carted off to Bangor to jail, then why was Chester Brown here? Dead. Why would they leave him and take everyone else? See, it doesn't make sense.

Also, I know it's only some squirrels waiting out the storm, just like me, but I sure wish they would stop walking around up there in the loft. The loft is where the ladder leads, the ladder Chester Brown broke his neck on. Every time I hear that rustling sound I think it's someone up there. Someone who killed Chester Brown, even though I know he just slipped and fell.

If only this storm would end. If only those squirrels would

shut up. If only...

The reason this part is blue is because that's Santa Clara's favorite color and I'm about to get around to when I met her.

This storm that's got me trapped reminds me of Chesuncook. Snow! You wouldn't believe the snow that winter I spent in the Allagash. One storm I remember lasted three days. Dear God, don't let this one last three days!

Danny got back from Australia the middle of March, same day as the starlings. He seemed relieved to find me alive and the camp in one piece. I showed him my water hole.

"Pretty good," he said, "this time a year." It still measured close to two feet across.

"You got any plans?" he asked.

It sounded a little like he was asking did I plan to leave that day or wait until morning. It wasn't as if I was so keen on staying. Just that I had no place else to go. No place else I wanted to go. Jaspers had invited me to the Catholic Worker house down on the Bowery and even Sister Marie Therese in a luke warm sort of way said I would be welcome there. But having lived through my baptism of ice and been born again into this new wilderness life, I had no intention of returning to New York City, not even to live on the Bowery.

To Danny I said, "No, not what you could call plans." I said, "I haven't thought about it much. Actually, all I've thought about is staying alive. If you want to know the truth, I didn't think this winter was ever gonna end."

"Oh," Danny laughed. "It ain't over yet!"

He hired me to help get the camps ready for summer. Minimum wage plus room and board, and it was charity really because what did I know about replacing sills, patching roofs, glazing windows. All I knew how to do was let my fingers do the walking, and at Chesuncook the only yellow pages were old newspapers city folk had left behind and Danny had saved for kindling or insulation. I should have paid him, because by June I had learned enough to get by.

Danny explained to me about getting by. "You still got New York syndrome," he said. "Always in a hurry to get somewhere and afraid someone else'll get there first. Still, none a you know where the hell you're goin', just racing along in someone else's dust. A bunch a lemmins is what you act like. Rush up here, get outta the rat race, then spend all your time turnin' this here into a rat race same as what you was gettin' away from in the first place. Take Maria."

I wished I could have. She hadn't written like she promised, or maybe during winter there just wasn't any mail to Chesuncook. I hadn't heard from anyone since November, not Maria, not the kids, no one.

"Maria," Danny said and sighed. He was still in love with her and it was going on four years since she left him. I hoped to heaven it wouldn't take me any four years to get over her. "Maria, she's always goin' on about us just gettin' by up here. You got no ambition, she says. You just get by. She says it's a way of life, gettin' by, like that was somethin' bad. I say what the hell, you don't find us runnin' down to New York City cause it's so wonderful down there. It's you comin' up here I told her, where we're gettin' by, and right off you start makin' it over like where you been and want to get away from. Now what the hell kinda sense does that make!"

I left Chesuncook when the black flies came, the end of May, with close to a thousand dollars in cash plus my own hammer and a Stanley retractable tape measure, all from Danny along with this advice: "You go on down to Disgusta and take a room there at the Augusta House. Then what you do is you put up little notices all over the place, like in the laundromats, and the super markets and the library. Say you do odd jobs. You'll get by, you'll see."

It seemed scary. It was scary. But I did it, and Danny was right. I got by.

But my first job I felt like an ass-hole. This old woman in Hallowell wanted me to rehang her kitchen door so it didn't stick. I'd hung doors with Danny before, but doing one on my own I forgot everything. Her name was Rose. She used to work in the mill down there on Water Street in Hallowell and she was on the security. You could tell she didn't have much. I guess she could tell I didn't have much either, not much money and not much experience. We struggled with the door together, her helping out with advice and a bowl of home-made chicken soup afterwards. We got to be friends. She said when I was done, handing me a five dollar bill, "You'll get by, Alex. Don't you worry."

The Augusta House—they tore it down a couple years later to make way for a bank—had seen better days, but even in its last years it had an air of elegance about it, like a grand old lady down on her luck. It stood on the rotary at the edge of town, a wide verandah—the natives called it a piazza—across the front. On Sunday afternoons that summer, I'd join the pensioners there and we would rock and neighbor and watch the tourists go round and round the circle. Sometimes we had a contest counting out-of-state license plates. One Sunday afternoon, sitting there rocking, I met Julie. She asked was I the one advertising to do odd jobs. She was young, in her twenties still, and looked like a dyke. In Maine that doesn't mean much, I had already discovered, since most women dress sensible. Still, Julie looked able to do her own odd jobs. I didn't get it.

"Yeah. That's me," I said. "Why."

"Julie Harris," she said, sticking out her hand. "Glad to meet you."

"Alex Adler," I replied and took her hand in mine. It was crusty with callus, warm and dry. It felt good in mine. Like competent. Like reliable. I held onto it a little too long think-ing about the texture of it, comparing it unconsciously to the feel of Maria's painter hands, so beautifully, so treacherous-ly soft.

Julie grinned and slid her hand free. "You interested in working our crew?" she asked. Direct, like her hands. She explained, "See, we landed this job, renovations on Sewall

Street, making it over into apartments. There're three of us, but we really need a fourth to get it done. We split even, like partners, but Terry and me, we take ten percent off the top. It's our equipment, see, the ladders, the skill saw, all that stuff. What do you think?"

I hesitated, my mind too full of my inadequacy to answer. Julie misunderstood. "You'll do ok. We generally clear a hundred fifty or so a week each. Under the table so it's all clear. Didn't figure you'd mind about the ten percent seein' how you're livin' in the Augusta House and all, it's not likely you got much in the way of equipment or anything."

"It's not that," I said. "It's..." How could I say that I really didn't know how to do carpentry?

A smile broke over Julie's face. "Great!" she exclaimed. "Then you'll do it."

"Well," I said and stopped. Then I thought of Danny and of Rose, both old-timers, real Maineacs, and them agreeing: "Alex, don't worry. You'll get by."

"Sure," I said. "I guess I could get by on that."

The renovation lasted through the winter. Right before Christmas I took a little one-room apartment with a Murphy bed on Sewall Street a block from where we were working so I didn't need a car. The A&P was still open there on State Street, three blocks away, next to Lithgow library. The furthest place I ever went to was the bar, Rosie's, on Water Street, Friday nights, Dyke night, and I always got a ride home with someone after. Julie and Terry were partners in more than business, so I never got to holding hands again. But Julie's simple presence was a comfort and before too long I really did earn my quarter share (minus ten percent off the top) of what the renovation paid.

January is when I first heard about Santa Clara. She was on TV one Friday night. I caught it at the bar. Channel VII, the local news out of Bangor. Santa Clara was explaining about a religious community called Rerum Novarum—this was before the name change—out on some island off the coast of Maine where they held what she kept calling inspirational work retreats. She was beautiful and all the dykes at Rosie's were hanging on every word she said. Close-up shots all you could see were her big black eyes. They seemed serene but at the same time sad, you felt somehow she was full of passion and mystery. Her eyes kind of came out of the television and locked onto your heart. Her head was framed, you might say cropped, by this black and white bandanna. Distance shots showed her dressed all in denim, denim overalls over a denim work shirt. Even her shoes looked to be denim sneakers. When the interview was over everyone started speculating—was she a dyke or wasn't she? Where Julie and me were Catholic, they started egging us on to take an inspirational work retreat with Sister Clara.

What we made out from the interview was for fifty dollars you could spend the weekend on this island, which everyone in the bar took to calling Rarin' to Go, and do about a hundred dollars worth of work for them logging, roofing, gardening, and stuff. The inspirational part happened on Saturday night and was Mass in Latin. Though everyone at Rosie's agreed Sister Clara was all the inspiration they were likely to need.

I was hearing regularly from the kids by then. Scott and Jennifer had visited at Christmas and I'd taken them skiing at Sugarloaf, borrowing Julie and Terry's car. The kids loved the Murphy bed. I slept on the floor. The end of July, Clarence Senior said all four could come for two weeks, he was going to Majorca. I didn't think all four would fit on the Murphy bed and when it was down, there was hardly floor room left for me. Soon as I found out they were coming, I started into worrying.

Julie said, "Alex, why don't you write Sister Clara and ask if you can bring the kids out there for a week." I could think of a dozen reasons why not. I said, "To my kids, work is a four letter word."

"So, they'll get their money's worth out of you. Main thing is it sounds like there's a lot for kids to do there, not like here in Augusta. So long as they keep busy and outta people's way."

"Yeah. And where'm I supposed to get two hundred and fifty dollars?"

"Write you're poor but your kids need inspiration. Hey! What's the harm in trying? All they can do is say no."

This was the first of June. We'd finished the Sewall Street renovations and were working on Winthrop Street making a lovely old home into an office block. A job to break your heart. I had a little money saved up, enough to put down on a car. On the solstice, (according to the KJ horoscope, it was a good day for new ventures) I picked up a VW bus some hippy had once owned and I wrote to Sister Clara asking could I bring four kids to Rerum Novarum. I listed all my get-by skills. I promised to do enough work for two and asked could we come for just one hundred dollars. I added we would camp and bring all our own food.

Julie was wrong when she said all they could do is say no. What happened is they never said anything. I didn't get my letter returned, and this was back when the postal service was still fairly reliable, so I decided they thought my request was too outrageous even to bother answering. The day before the kids arrived I bought a second-hand tent and decided to take them to Baxter State Park.

About the Murphy bed sleeping four. I was right and I was wrong. Scott and Jennifer had talked it up big, this bed you pulled down from the wall. Clary and Timothy had their hearts set on it; as did Scott and Jennifer. So, all four kids spent the night on the Murphy bed, but none of us got any sleep to speak of. About four in the morning, it was already light, we hung it up and walked out Winthrop Street to the airport where we watched planes come in until the Corner Restaurant opened, when we walked back down the hill to breakfast.

After breakfast we had a big fight. It broke out on Winthrop Street in front of the building we were turning into an office block. Julie and Terry were there and they intervened; they kind of refereed us. Scott was thrilled at the idea of camping at Baxter, he wanted to climb Mt. Katadhin, which is the northern terminus of the Appalachian Trail. This preference of Scott's prompted Jennifer to say she'd rather go anywhere in the world than Baxter State Park because it was nasty. She refused to elucidate. Clary and Timothy just kept saying they were goin' fishin' and they could care less what the rest of us did.

Julie said, "Take them to Rarin' to Go."

This caught all five of us completely off guard. We all repeated it, Rarin' to Go, as if we thought it was a good idea or something. Then I said, "We can't go there. They never even answered my letter."

This, of course, united the opposition. "We want to go to Rarin' to Go!" The kids started dancing up and down. "Rarin' to Go! Rarin' to Go!"

"Go," said Julie. "Just go."

"What about the little fact they never answered my letter?" I asked.

"They're just flakes," she said.

"They're probably full."

"Who," asked Julie, "would pay fifty dollars for a chance to work their buns off and use an out-house? Trust me. Nobody's there. Go."

After the word out-house there was no way to get out of it. The kids had made up their minds and for once they were in agreement.

Santa Clara, chain-saw in hand, was standing at the end of the sand spit when we drove up. Except for her blue shirt being polished cotton instead of denim, she looked just the same as she had on television.

"Welcome," she said. "We've been waiting for you."

Chapter Six—Green

Willow, willow, sing all a green willow.

I knew the second I saw her I had known her before. Not in this life, but in several other ones. We kept looking at each other until Jennifer poked me in the ribs and said, "Well, are we gonna go across or not?"

It turned out to be a line, that "Welcome, we've been waiting for you." Santa Clara read it somewhere like in the Catholic Worker paper and it caught her fancy. When they decided to try to raise some money with inspirational work retreats, she schooled everyone to say it. But until I came along, no one had had a chance to. And when the moment came, when this tired old VW bus filled with kids and painted psychedelic pink with silver trim came bumping down the rutted field road to the spit, Santa Clara very nearly said, "Sugar! What do you want?"

I'm glad she caught herself, because if she had said that, I would have turned around and driven right out of there and my life would have been a whole lot less interesting than it has been.

Take this body on the couch for instance. If it weren't for Santa Clara and her refugees, none of this would have happened to me. I would never have been followed by Chester Brown for weeks as I was, and I wouldn't be here now. At least not with him dead on the couch over there. About an hour ago he moved. Frightened! thought I'd die. Every once in a while he twitches. I took a look, and he is truly dead. I figure it must be rigor mortis. If it gets much colder, rigor mortis will be setting in on me too. I wish it would set in on those damn squirrels upstairs. They'll be quiet and I forget they're there. Then it sounds just like someone on the floor shifting in their sleep. Plus, I never heard a squirrel sneeze before. But in this cold anyone might sneeze. I have, why not a squirrel.

My first night alone out to Chesuncook, after Danny left, I went and read *In Cold Blood*. Pretty stupid thing to do. I heard people moving around all that night, too, and couldn't sleep.

It's a good thing Sister Benedict keeps an emergency supply of beans on hand. As soon as it's light I'll haul in more wood and start melting snow. There's plenty of it. I do wish this storm would start to wind down soon. But I'm afraid it reminds me of that one at Chesuncook, the one that lasted three days.

My first words to Santa Clara, I'm talking in this life, were, "Oh, so you did get my letter."

"Who are you?" she said.

I felt confused.

"I thought you just said," I started, but Jennifer was talking louder and more to the point.

"I'm Jennifer Miller, and this is my mother, her name is Alex, well, Alexandra, really, but everyone calls her Alex, and those guys in the back, they're my brothers. Are you Sister Clara? We've come to work."

At the mention of work, Santa Clara lightened up considerably. "Oh, welcome!"

You could tell she was about to say we've been waiting for you, again, but she caught herself and said instead, "I'm waiting for a load of hay. You didn't see an old green Chevy truck broke down, did you?"

Scott sniggered in my ear, "She needs glasses if she thought we were a load of hay."

Jennifer said, "No, we did not. Do you want me to stay here and wait with you?"

Looking a little to the left of my ear, Santa Clara said, "Did you come for the retreat?"

I started to babble. "I know you're probably full, but the kids had their hearts set on it, so I thought at least they could see the place, they're city kids..."

But Jennifer coolly overrode me. "She wrote you, but probably you didn't get the letter. She often forgets to mail them. No one could have that bad luck with the mails. But she is a terrific carpenter. And we always help her with everything. You should see the work she does in Augusta. That's the capital." She added this cachet self importantly. Jennifer was twelve going on thirty. "Isn't that right, Alex?" She said this less for confirmation than to introduce me into the negotiations.

Santa Clara's eyes briefly touched mine. "They call you Alex?" she asked and then her eyes took off again, roaming the distance between my ear and the sky. I longed to have them rest a while in mine the way they had when we first drove up.

Scott, behind me, yelled, "Alex. Mom. It doesn't matter. She says call her anything, just don't call her late for supper." He threw himself back in the seat and started gagging and guffawing.

New people still affect Scott that way, especially if he's attracted to them. He was only eleven and if he was going on anything, it was ten. Clary and Timothy are twins and they would be ten in September.

Addressing the overhead light, Santa Clara said; "We sure could use a carpenter. How long can you stay?"

Jennifer said, "Two weeks."

Santa Clara looked at her fully, engaging both eyes, and I felt a twinge of envy. "Do you have a tent?" she asked.

"Can we go fishing?" Clary and Tim inquired together. "If we can't," one of them said. "We're not staying," said the other.

"Oh Christ," muttered Scott, in my ear again, "do you believe those two?"

Jennifer said to Santa Clara, "They'll stay all right, don't worry, but if they could fish, it would keep them outta our hair."

"They can fish for mackerel off the pier," said Santa Clara. She laughed. When she laughs, you can see her teeth, they're big and white and her lips are full and soft. She laid her hand on the car door, her fingers resting half inside, inches from my shoulder. The nails were short and soiled with earth. She saw me notice them and said, "Peasant hands." And I believed her, caught in the romance of it, because in fact they were the hands of a patrician, not a peasant, long fingered and perfectly formed, the calluses and the dirt lying on them like merit badges. I saw her look at my hands resting on the wheel, clean and filed, cuticles soft and trimmed, kept like my mother taught me, like I was teaching Jennifer. And I felt ashamed of them.

Scott piped up, "You should see Mom's calluses. Man! They are humongous!"

"So, she really is a carpenter," Santa Clara said to Scott who started to gag again. "Scott, would you like to wait with me for the hay?"

Her eyes touched mine briefly. "If you drive across the spit, you'll be stuck on the island until the next low tide. Do you mind?"

I told her no, I didn't mind. I didn't tell her I wouldn't mind if I got stuck there forever so long as she was there and just once in a while would let her eyes rest in mine.

"Well, go on in. Put your tent up wherever you like. There's only Sister Barbara and Father Frank here now. If you see them, introduce yourself. If you follow the stream down to the bay the pier is right there. Be careful you don't fall in," she said to the twins. "Scott and I will come in on the hay truck, if it ever gets here."

"Scott, you coming?" she asked.

Scott seemed to levitate out the door. Jennifer put as good face on it as she could. All she said, half way across the spit, was, "I just hope Scott doesn't blow it. Oh well, I did offer to be the one to stay."

It was good, I reflected, that the hearts of two of us at least were pure. All Clary and Tim wanted from the week was the chance to catch fish, the kind with fins and scales.

There was something both crazy and appealing about life on the island. Mostly it made no sense to me: Why would a bunch of educated, middle to upper class people want to go bury themselves in such uncomfortable circumstances as those on Rerum Novarum, or Monte Cassino as it was soon to be called. Now, you might say the same about me, being a handyman and all in Disgusta, Maine. But I didn't quite choose my lot. I was only getting by, not making a Kantian statement out of my calluses and my Murphy bed.

We sat around on the floor of Trinity after Mass our last Saturday there. Father Frank, Barbara, Clara and I, finishing off the half gallon of Wild Irish Rose they used for Mass, Scott and Jennifer making free with cider I suspect had begun to turn.

Scott said, he was sitting back behind the wood stove out sight, "I like it here."

"Me too," said Jennifer, "but I wouldn't want to live here. No way."

Scott started gagging.

Father Frank asked, "Why is that?"

"Lots of reasons," said Jennifer.

Jennifer was too old for ca-ca jokes and not old enough to take the alimentary canal and its functions in stride. What makes me think the cider had started to go is she said, "Like take one example, going to the out-house in the middle of winter."

"Oh Christ!" Scott moaned. "Let me outta here."

"Yeah," said Father Frank. "That bothered me too before I came. But it's not that bad really. When you gotta go, you gotta go."

"Oh my god," from Scott, still behind the woodstove.

"What else," asked Santa Clara, "bothers you, Jennifer?"

"Well, like the whole thing. I mean, you never go to the movies. Or get dressed up. You know. Go out to dinner. Like have fun. I mean, I really do like it here. Don't get me wrong. But. You know what I mean?"

Then Santa Clara launched into a monologue. That was the first time I heard it. She began with the power of intercessionary prayer. As she talked, Sister Barbara, enraptured, seemed to glow with attention and Scott edged out from behind the stove, just his head, so he could watch her.

Unless you've already come across a truly charismatic person, there simply is no way to suggest the attractive power of their personality adequately. No more than there is a way to defend yourself against it, though some people seem to have a natural immunity. Take Father Frank, for instance. He was clearly bored by Santa Clara and her monologue and he used the interlude to finish off the bottle of wine. But the rest of us were hooked.

After touching on intercessionary prayer, Santa Clara began some Midrash on Peter Maurin and that peasant scholasticism he brought to the Catholic Worker movement.

Mongrel daughter of a Sicilian mother and a Jewish intellectual from Vienna, I knew about Midrash as well as I knew the details of each appearance Mary had made since her assumption some two thousand years ago. My father had heaped disdain on both. Midrash, Jewish commentaries on Hebrew scriptures, he described as claptrap when he didn't call them something worse. When Mother began to talk about Guadalupe or Lourdes, Dad would only snort and rattle his newspaper. It was easy for me, when I left home, to wean myself from the ceremonies of Mass and confession and other superstitions. But at college, I studied Medieval history, sorting out as best I could the contradictory currents of my psyche.

Peter Maurin, like other Catholic positivists, and like the encyclical Rerum Novarum, has a liberal veneer covering a reactionary heart. That was Dad's judgement, and I share it. They sound good, but their words don't stand up to scrutiny, especially historical scrutiny: too many became fascists in the thirties; they started the Falange in Spain, rose to power in Opus Dei.

But hearing the words spoken is different from reading them. Listening to Santa Clara there on the floor of Trinity, my belly warm with the fruit of the vine, my muscles aching pleasantly from the work of my hands building a stall for her cow, mesmerized by the soft spell of her voice, enchanted with desire to have her eyes come back to mine, then I wanted to believe. And why not? What was wrong with this image of life Santa Clara drew with her words on the still summer air? Of a people returned to the land, living in humble communities like Rerum Novarum, living simply so others could simply live. Bound together by a faith so strong that they were able to transcend all base emotions like greed, and envy, and lust. Living together to promote the well-being of others, finding in each person a reflection of God, encountering in the stranger the figure of Jesus outside Emmaus.

Father Frank's vinous snores brought us back to the reality of approaching night, dirty dishes, and the need to haul water before dark.

The next day, our last full day on the island, Sister Benedict showed up late in the afternoon. She arrived with a ton of newsprint, pastels, charcoal and water colors. Farmer Drinkwater's son, Rudy, brought the load across the spit on his tractor. Santa Clara and Sister Barbara, with Scott tagging along behind as usual, came out of the woods just as he was leaving, the art supplies piled outside the cabin, that original ten-by-twelve shed, where Santa Clara and Sister

Benedict still lived.

"What's this?" asked Santa Clara at Rudy's departing back. The tractor was puffing diesel smoke and making a terrible racket. If he heard the question, Rudy was choosing to ignore it.

"Wow!" said Scott, who loves to draw, "Get a load of this!"

Sister Benedict appeared in the door of the cabin, "They're mine," she said.

Jennifer and I had spent the past several days building an extension on the lean-to to house a cow Santa Clara had in mind to buy. We were taking a break when the tractor arrived with the gross of newsprint and other art supplies. In fact, we helped to unload it. I hadn't realized Sister Benedict was in the cabin until she appeared in the doorway to say, "They're mine."

The air between Sister Benedict and Santa Clara was immediately charged, like gasses in a bell jar. Startled, Sister Barbara scuttled up the path to St. Anne and Scott went flying down the road to the pier. Jennifer and I sat perfectly still just out of range.

"Take them to the barn," said Santa Clara. "There's no room for them in the cabin."

"I made room," said Sister Benedict. She opened wide the door revealing a pile of denim clothing, boots and a stack of books. "That's my stuff," said Santa Clara.

"Take them to the barn," said Sister Benedict, "There's no room for them in my cabin."

Santa Clara, for years, pondered the injury of her eviction, and she determined to mend her ways. Ever after, Santa Clara made her title of ownership clear to whomever she might be living with. This I know from experience, but that comes later in my story. If any evicting was to be done, Santa Clara made sure, from that time forward, that she would be the one to do it. I know.

Scott helped Santa Clara move her belongings into the barn. Jennifer and I knocked together some shelves in the cow stall and built a bed for her mattress. Even Clary and Tim showed some solidarity bringing in six good sized mackerel, gutted, as an offering for dinner which Santa Clara shared with us at our camp fire.

Scott said, "That lady must be some artist."

But Santa Clara didn't answer him. I found out later she called what she was doing meditating. Clary and Timothy were mesmerized by her mole which seemed in the light of our fire to glow. I was fascinated by it too, but I tried not to stare. Around eight o'clock, Santa Clara said she thought she would go check up on things. She moseyed down the path to St. Anne and Sister Barbara. Whatever she found there took a lot of checking, because she hadn't come back yet when we put out the fire and turned in for the night.

Low tide was six in the morning, so we were up and out of there early. Breaking camp in the pale light of dawn, we imagined everyone was still asleep and we kept whispering to each other, except when someone got mad, and then the rest of us would all go SHHH! loud enough to wake the dead. But it turned out we were the last ones up. On our way out, we heard that duet of Santa Clara and Sister Barbara off in the woods.

"I wish I'd got to say good-by," said Scott wistfully when he heard the buzz of their chainsaws.

We met Father Frank jogging across the spit, and on the other side, there was Sister Benedict sketching. I only caught sight of it out the corner of my eye, but all it looked like was a bunch of angry black lines.

Chapter Seven—Santa Clara (Blues)

During the next few years, I read about Santa Clara every once in a while in the *KJ*, Augusta's newspaper, the *Kennebec Journal*. And she had occasion to read about me in the *Bangor Daily*. I'm not sure which stories were more edifying. It depends, I guess, on your point of view. They were different. I mean they both were different.

What happened on the island, now called Monte Cassino, is that someone was healed. The story's not real clear, whether it was the water from the spring or the laying on of hands, whether it was through the intercession of Mary or of Joseph. But on these facts, everyone agrees: an old woman from Dedham saw Santa Clara on television one night talking about the power of intercessionary prayer. Afterwards, in a dream, someone spoke to her, (there is some confusion: was it Mary talking or Joseph?) and said for her to bring her granddaughter, who suffered from cerebral palsy, to Santa Clara to be healed. It was in all the papers when, according to the grandmother, little Ellen rose from her wheelchair and walked.

"It was just like Jesus," the old woman said. "Sister said to me, 'The child is healed. Go, and don't tell no one.'"

But tell she did. She explained that the good Lord, in another dream, admonished her, saying, "Spread the Good News."

All Santa Clara would say was "no comment."

I guess for a while a lot of people went to the island, when the tide was out, looking for something, a cure, an inspiration, relief from the tedium of a winter day. They all were greeted with "Welcome, we've been waiting for you," and a list of jobs to choose from: roofing St. Anne, splitting wood, hauling water, mucking out the barn. Most turned away. Some few stayed. Santa Clara's reputation grew, but not so much as a healer, for there remained some doubt and confusion about that, though every once in a while a cure was proclaimed and someone enjoyed Warhol's allotted fifteen minutes of fame. No, her reputation grew as the leader of "an extraordinary spiritual community on an island off the coast of Maine. Named Monte Cassino, it is reminiscent of a Medieval ascetic community." Or so the blurb ran in the *AAA Travel Guide* for tourists to that part of Downeast Maine. The first year the words were 'Medieval mendicant community,' but because begging ran counter to Peter Maurin's philosophy of self-sufficiency, (if not counter to reality, for the community still relied heavily on gifts from Central America via Sister Benedict's family, and from local businesses via unpaid bills), Santa Clara insisted in subsequent editions of the *Travel Guide* that the word ascetic replace mendicant. It should be noted that, within reason, local creditors were easy about Monte Cassino's unpaid bills, discounting them against the greatly increased tourist trade of the religiously curious. And the curiously religious, though the latter, mostly long-haired and drug dependent, the locals would just as soon have done without as they tended not to spend much money.

Time for red again

The red's for me. Red Adler. This is how I got into the news twice in the years after our visit to Monte Cassino. Just remembering makes me wonder whether my dead pal there in the quilt could possibly have been with the FBI. I don't think so. Chester Brown, if that's his name, was with the

INS. I'm almost positive. It was the Central American refugees that Santa Clara and Maria kept slipping across the border into Canada that got his nose out of joint.

Question: Do squirrels snore?

Back to the '70s. After they killed those students at Kent State and Jackson State, there was a burst of political activism in Maine, especially with the VVAW and a group called SCAR who were into prison reform. One man, a working-class Franco-American from Saco, was the driving force behind both organizations. I met him one Sunday afternoon in spring.

Some of us, delegates to the State Democratic Convention in 1972, were meeting in Lithgow Library to plan platform strategy when in barges a man about five-ten or eleven, jeans torn there at the knee, hair pulled back in a ponytail, scar running across one eyebrow. "You can't do this!" he explained, vigorously thumping the table and scowling ferociously, the scar running through his eyebrow livid.

"Right!" I said.

I was leading the meeting so it was me he was thumping at.

"Right," I urged. "Let's wrap it up, you guys!"

But Julie stopped me. "Bull shit!" she said. "Who are you and what the hell do you mean we can't do what?"

She told me later what she saw when he came storming through the door were his eyes. "They're the softest blue eyes," Julie said. "I knew he was just a teddy bear."

The teddy bear turned to Julie. "This is crap," he said. "What we need is a demo outside the convention site. This is what you gotta do."

His plans included a speech by me. He told me I could say what I liked, but it better have a lot to do with an Administration that murders peasants on the other side of the world and its own youth at home. I agreed. Tell me who wouldn't.

Next day this story appeared in all the papers.

Former Instructor Denounces Government

Alexandra Adler, political activist and former history instructor from New York City, spoke in Vassalboro yesterday during a march to protest the Administration's policy in Vietnam. Ms. Adler arrived in Maine the day before the march, coming from Charlotte, North Carolina, where she was a defendant in the trial of the Charlotte vice squad.

The charges stemmed from an incident three years previously when Ms. Adler and her companion, Ms. Maria Papandreou, in Charlotte on a visit, had their hotel room searched and were questioned by the Charlotte vice squad.

Talk about intimidation, innuendo, and downright lies. The vice squad was on trial, not me. Maria and I were among the plaintiffs pressing charges. Mr. Annum had sent us tickets to come. It had been close on four years since I saw Maria last, leaving Chesuncook with that big Swede, Maj.

We talked on the phone right before the trial. She was alone, she told me; Maj turned over lovers as frequently as shrinks.

It isn't true I had gotten over Maria. Not quite anyway. But enough so I knew better than to start something down there in Charlotte. Besides, I had the kids to keep me busy. All of us went to the movies together both nights. During the day, being in court kept me out of mischief.

Scott, as it turned out, was mixed up in a law-suit of his own. Henry Kissinger had visited Charlotte a few months before, and Scott had joined the protesters. He sold copies of his Quaker Sunday School paper with articles by himself and a couple other kids denouncing the war. He was among dozens who were arrested. We both won our cases, though Scott's wasn't settled until after the war was over. A fat lot of good winning did either of us. The vice squad continued to poh-leece as it always had in Charlotte. And, like they say, El Salvador is Spanish for Vietnam.

CHAPTER EIGHT—LAVENDER

Lavender as in triangles and, Lavender's blue, dilly dilly.

The second time I made the papers, a few years later, 1980 or so, it was when I spoke at the Unitarian church there in Augusta. The minister had asked me to talk about the problems of being homosexual. Like I told him, being homosexual isn't a problem. The problem is homophobia. I thought I made this real clear.

"Which is it?" I asked the congregation. "The Jewish problem, or anti-Semitism? Is it the Race Problem, or is racism the problem?" And finally, I asked, "Is the problem being homosexual, or is the problem homophobia?"

The congregation got two of these three questions right. But getting one wrong made them spleeny.

This appeared in Monday's paper:

Problems of Being Homosexual

Augusta lesbian, Alexandra Adler, spoke yesterday to a congregation at the Unitarian Church in Augusta about the problem of being a homosexual.

The rest of the story was about as accurate as the lead. Except for some personal information like where I lived in Augusta which they got letter perfect.

Monday afternoon my landlord came by and gave me two days' notice. Actually, worse things had happened to me in my life. For all its being romantic, I never did like that Murphy bed.

And I got a lot of phone calls, not all of them unfriendly. I finally changed to an unlisted number, but not before I got this call from Santa Clara.

She said, "Alex how are you?" and a few things like that. She never came right out and said she'd read about me, but come on, that's a big coincidence when I hadn't heard from her once since our visit ten years before. I asked her about the others, Father Frank and Sister Agnes. I asked if she ever got the cow we made the stall for. She said no she was still sleeping there. Then all of a sudden she says, "I would like to talk with you."

"Well, sure," I said. "Of course."

The funniest thing popped into my head that Santa Clara was pregnant. Which I knew was nonsense because, parthenogenesis aside, I do not believe in virgin births.

It was mid-April, my first date with Santa Clara. We met at Jordan's on Route One in Searsport. I planned to take her to dinner but she said she wasn't hungry. She said, "Do you think we could go for a ride?" She wanted to talk. In private.

She dropped her bombshell as we sat in the fog, parked at Lamoine Beach. You couldn't see a thing, the fog was so thick. Looking steadily into it, she said, "I'm attracted to you."

She could have sounded happier saying, "I've got terminal cancer. Two weeks to live."

I said, "Oh."

It didn't make much sense to me, us sitting there in the fog, her saying it straight out like that, sounding so sad, not looking at me. Also, in the dark, I couldn't see her eyes, the potent source of her attractive power. The silence got awkward, and so I said, "Well, what do you want to do about it?"

Not the most romantic answer in the world, but Santa Clara didn't seem to mind. Right away she said, "Does our relationship have to be...?"

And that's how it started, this weird way I do all the talking for us both whenever we have what you might, for want of a better word, call a conversation.

She didn't say anything more, just, "Does our relationship have to be...?"

After a long time sitting there in the dark, not able to see her eyes, not that she was looking my way, I said, "I guess you're asking does a relationship between us have to be sexual."

She still said nothing. It wasn't until long afterwards that I even thought about the fact I might have used this opportunity to consider whether I wanted a relationship with this odd woman who, when she spoke, spoke 'Midrash' and was so devastatingly attractive at least when you could see her eyes. But I didn't. I was too busy figuring out what she needed to say and for some reason couldn't. Then saying it for her, ever so careful to get it right; and then responding, not to my needs, but to hers as I imagined them to be. It was not unlike playing gin rummy with yourself, but with this difference: I kept subordinating my hand to the dummy's.

After a while I answered myself. I said, no it doesn't, it doesn't have to be sexual, but, I pointed out, to be scrupulously fair, most likely it would turn out to be.

After another little while I said maybe she was getting cold and would just as soon go back to Searsport. Since she didn't say anything, that's what we decided to do.

The last thing we decided that night was she would come visit me for a weekend the middle of May.

I said, "Maybe you're nervous about my apartment. I want you to know I have two bedrooms."

What I didn't tell her is I had only one bed. But I figured in three weeks I could manage to find another bed, one I could afford, plus bedding for it. I didn't like to ask her to bring a sleeping bag.

When we said good-bye, I reached over and planted a little kiss on her ear. But if she felt it, she didn't give herself away.

I bought a foam mattress and a metal bed frame. There was no way I could afford a box spring, so at Grossman's I picked up a piece of that wafer board and cut it to size. I used the scraps to make a bedside table and bought a lamp on special at LaVerdiere's for $9.95. That Friday afternoon I picked some lilac and put it by her bed in a mayonnaise jar alongside a volume of Gerard Manley Hopkins.

I'm providing all these details about how I fixed up Santa Clara's room which is silly because she never saw it. What happened is, we were in the living room after supper. This is a big apartment, and I didn't have any furniture, so we were sitting on my two kitchen chairs. She was drying her hair, which I'd never really seen before, just wisps of it escaping from the black and white bandanna she always wore like a coif. It's amazing how deeply red her hair is. It's long and thick as a horse's tail, wiry like that, and beautiful. She kept running her fingers through it, then tossing her head so the hair would fan out, then settle again over her shoulders. She wore a long flannel nightgown with a blue ribbon around the yoke and a pair of mukluks on her feet. She looked about twenty, and it was hard to think of her wandering around in the woods with her chainsaw knocking down trees.

I was kind of talking for both of us and finding it hard to concentrate on what we were saying.

I told her about the renovation we were doing down on Winthrop Street. Then I answered myself. "It probably seems funny to you us building with new material and all, the way you work out to Monte Cassino using slab wood and resawn." Pursuing this theme from my perspective, I pointed out you don't really save money using poor material. "It takes longer for one thing," I said. "And for another, probably it won't last as long."

Seeing the flaws in that argument, flaws from her point of view, after a moment I said, "Of course the way you see it, probably, is what you have a lot of is time and you're short on money. Besides, it really isn't so much how long resawn lasts, it's more a question of how it looks. And out there at Monte Cassino, you stop to think about it, resawn's every bit as good as planed. Better even. Like it's more in keeping."

Santa Clara all this time kept running her fingers through her hair and tossing her head. And she kept looking blank, her eyes fixed on some middle distance a little to the right of my ear. It can get unnerving. But that night it filled me with a complicated desire. She was the sleeping princess my kiss might wake.

It took years for me to accept that, for me at least, she was the mountain made of glass I would never climb. The sweet mysteries her eyes promised, were safe from me. That night I didn't know I was only one of many who had tried to penetrate those defenses raised in childhood. It wouldn't have mattered. I always identified with the hero who broke through the brambles, rode boldly up the slippery slope, slew the giant for the golden egg. I was in lust and it was her sweet aloofness, that crystal exterior, those glimpses of a soul under glass, that spurred my desire.

Along about nine o'clock I said, "I'm tired. You must be tired too, working all day, and that drive. It must have taken you nearly three hours." Then I heard myself say, "I got your room fixed up, but maybe you'd just as soon sleep with me."

For the life of me I can't remember her saying a word one way or another. But this I do know: Santa Clara never laid eyes on the room in that apartment which I think of to this day as Santa Clara's bedroom.

And another thing: Maybe she didn't talk much when she was sitting down or standing up, but it was a whole different story when lying down. You could say she found her tongue then.

The morning after was awfully sweet as those first mornings almost always are and while still in bed, Santa Clara managed to say, in a low husky voice, that she thought being with me forever was just about the right amount of time.

CHAPTER NINE—PINK

Pink, pink, you're a fink. Wash your feet so they don't stink.

Pink, I think, is a wishy-washy sort of color and, color-wise, it's the closest I can get to that first weekend of my life with Santa Clara.

Maybe it was the bacon. Neither of us eat much meat, but I got it for a treat and we really did eat too much of it. Anyway, I know it gave me indigestion. Plus the fact that we got hardly any sleep. After breakfast we both seemed to be a little sad. Not that she said anything.

I said, "Too bad it's raining. I bet you'd like to take a walk or something. Where you spend so much time outdoors, I mean."

She was sitting in the living room on a kitchen chair, staring out the window at the rain, at the maple tree in front. The tree looked Japanese, twigs and branches black like lacquer, and a chartreuse wash of new leaves and pollen. Her thick, red hair still was loose, but she had on her overalls, her blue denim work shirt, and her steel-toed boots. She didn't say a thing.

I said, "I shouldn't have cooked so much bacon."

I said, after a while, "I have baking soda."

And then I said, "I meant to get some Tums, but I forgot. But baking soda's real good. If you have indigestion."

I paused before adding, "I think I'll have some baking soda. Can I fix you some?"

That's when she said, "In Rockport, outside Boston's a Jesuit Retreat Center. I'm going. For spiritual advice."

She looked at me.

There's something funny about Clara's eyes. I always thought of them as dark brown. The reason is, whenever I did manage to make eye contact, I'd feel like I was falling into them. Falling into some deep well. Something cosmic. Something karmic. It felt...personal. Like I was going through her eyes and arriving at my own beginnings, finding my soul by passing through hers. This feeling was enhanced because she almost never looked at me. She'd look past me. Past my ear. Over my head. I'd get to wondering if she was mad at me. Pretty soon, all I'd be thinking about's her eyes and longing to plunge into them.

Then zap! There'd be this connection and I'd feel, while it lasted, tuned into eternity.

So afterwards, it would seem like her eyes were dark brown, maybe even black. But they're not. They're really hazel, a kind of yellow brown. But her lashes are dark and thick. Her brows are too, and serene.

But don't forget about that mole with the little red veins feeding into it, there by her nose like a third eye. It glows when she's mad.

She looked at me and she said, "Would you like to go with me?"

I said, "Sure." Enchanted. She perked right up. She even looked me in the eye and smiled, a sweet, shy smile, the way she had before breakfast when she told me she thought forever sounded about right for how long she wanted to be with me.

On the way down to Rockport, every once in a while Santa Clara cast a look in my direction. She even once or twice supplied her own answer to a question I asked. For instance: "What's this guy's name?" I said.

"Who?"

"This person you're going to see."

"It's a priest."

"This priest you're going to see."

"I don't know."

"You don't know?"

"Well, I know his name."

"Oh."

And then a little later I said, "Have you ever been to see him before?"

"Who?"

"This guy you're going to see."

"It's a priest."

"This priest you're going to see."

"No."

Dressed to seek spiritual guidance, Santa Clara looks much the same as when she lays waste to a forest. Black and white bandanna like a coif covering her head, a blue turtleneck, blue work shirt, blue overalls, steel-toed boots, plus a heavy duty iron crucifix on a leather thong. I noticed she kept hold of this crucifix most of the way down, something, I was to discover, she did when she felt stressed.

She didn't say anything when I asked if she sought spiritual advice often. So I carried that conversation on a while by myself, pausing periodically, the way you do, when someone's there.

I said, "My family doesn't go in for that sort of thing much. I mean we went to confession, of course, mother and me. But not for spiritual advice. Like, we never had the priest to dinner. That's what Protestants did...Probably your family was more religious. Being Irish...My family's mixed, ethnically speaking. My mom's from Sicily, well, her parents. Dad, he was, I guess you'd say he was agnostic. So, I'm a cradle Catholic, but maybe it was closer to being brought up Protestant...I think. Except we never had the priest to dinner."

During this disjointed conversation I was having with myself, I thought about Maj for some reason, the woman Maria went off with. I thought about Maj and her shrinks and the nutty way she used their advice. I remembered how Maj changed lovers and shrinks with the same regularity. I said, "How'd you hear about this...priest?"

She said, "Sister Benedict."

I took Clara's hand in mine. It was like trying to hold an empty glove. I let it go. I said, "Are you upset? About us I mean. Is that why you're going?"

She said, "No."

I said, "So you're just going to see this guy in general?"

She said, "He's a priest."

I said, "I know he's a priest. This priest. You're just going in general? Not because you're upset or anything?" She didn't answer and after a while I said, "Hello?" She jumped, like I'd startled her. I said, "Say what?"

She said, "What?"

I said, "Do you like Gerard Manley Hopkins?" Then after a while I said, "Probably you do. I noticed most of your books are by Catholics. Though maybe you think where he mostly wasn't supposed to be writing poetry, he should have obeyed orders.

"But I think those gifts are from God and it's like disobeying Her not to develop them.

"Maybe, though, you think that's just willfulness.

"I noticed you had some Christopher Dawson. Have you ever read Pirenne?" And so I prattled on for both of us until we got to Rockport.

The retreat center looked like a fancy resort there on the sea. While Santa Clara got her spiritual advice, I wandered around on the beach and skipped stones. She was gone a couple of hours. During those two hours, I did some thinking, reflecting on my Catholic girlhood mostly. Remembering how I had spent my life distancing myself from it. Along about four-thirty an off-shore breeze blew up and it got cold, so I went to wait in the car. While I sat there with nothing to do but worry, white-collared priests arrived and departed in Volvos and Hondas, and once in a while a Mercedes drove up to discharge a matron with cinnamon colored hair.

It was close to five when Santa Clara emerged from the mansion retreat. She stood for a moment on the marble terrace surveying the world. She seemed at peace. I got out of the car and waved. She didn't exactly wave back, just kind of fanned her fingers out from her side, and started toward me. When Santa Clara looks serene, which she quite often does, she seems like an old soul, old in the Hindu sense, a soul with a lot of practice, a soul on the homestretch toward Nirvana. She looked, as she approached the car, a notch or two beyond serene and moving into blissful.

"Well," I said, "that must have been a terrific session. You look great." She looked me fully in the eye. Zap! There I was in the middle of this parking lot but tuned into eternity, my soul mated with hers in a forever present that had always been and forever would be. On the highway heading home, I got around to asking, "So, how'd it go?"

"Good," said Santa Clara.

"Did you ask his advice about us?" I wanted to know.

"Yes."

I couldn't see how to conduct this conversation on my own, so after a while I said, "What'd he say? You seemed awfully happy, real serene when you came out of there."

"Yes," said Santa Clara.

"So you are happy?"

"Yes."

"He didn't say you were going to hell?"

"He said I shouldn't worry.

"Oh good."

"He said being in love is funny," she volunteered.

Well, that's for sure. "What'd he have in mind?" I asked.

"He said I might wake up in the morning and not even be in love. This problem just might take care of itself."

After a while I said, "Well whoop-de-doo." And that's all I said for the next three hours. Talk about meditating. What I was meditating on was getting Santa Clara out of my life. Out of my apartment. Out of my hair! Curiously, I never gave my heart a thought. Maybe because I was too angry. Also, I didn't think she'd been there long enough to take up residence.

Soon as we arrived in Augusta, Santa Clara announced she was heading back to Monte Cassino. That's when I lost it. "Whatta ya mean, goin' back to Monte Cassino," is how I started. "I just spent my Saturday driving you five-hundred fucking miles to see some Jesuit asshole and now you tell me you're leaving?"

A little smile began to play in the corners of her mouth, coming out and going in again. I was to learn this smile did not mean Santa Clara was amused. Far from it. But back then, not knowing any better, I thought she was laughing at my distress. My anger kicked into high gear. "Terrific! What is it you said this morning? Forever? Yeah, forever. 'I think being with you forever is just about right.'

"Forever unless you get lucky. Then maybe tomorrow morning, maybe then'll be long enough. Maybe then you won't be in love. Won't that be wonderful!!

"Hey, Clara! that's really terrific advice. Real spiritual. Fucking Jesuit asshole!" I continued ranting and Santa Clara continued smiling, but that third eye, that mole with the little red veins feeding into it, had started to glow. I noticed, but I was too far gone to pay attention.

Santa Clara got out of the car. She gently closed the door. Santa Clara, except for that fiery mole, looking sweet and fine as cotton candy, walked humbly in the gutter to the house. She kept her eyes downcast. At the door she waited, to one side, her hands held lightly clasped to her chest as if in prayer. I got the apartment door open okay, but shutting it, the whole house shook. Santa Clara just seemed to get smaller and humbler and since I couldn't see her face—she kept it down like I might hit her or something—I couldn't see her mole, which was really a lot more threatening, if you knew Santa Clara, than all my raving.

She said, before she left, that she didn't know why I was angry. She said, later, and often, that I flew into rages for no reason at all. I came to understand that for Santa Clara, the context of an argument began with my contribution to it— and after hers, which therefore, never counted. And then, of course, once things got going, I'd quickly escalate from rowdy to outrageous while she'd slide from quiet to submissively silent. While I raged a little more about Jesuits, she stood looking mournful by the door, her eyes cast heavenward, demure, like those cards they give you in catechism class: Santa Clara about to undergo martyrdom at the hands of the infidel. And then she left. I'd just spent three hours imagining how I was going to get rid of this woman. Once she left, I realized I would do anything to get her back again.

Chapter Ten—Green

The owl and the pussy cat went to sea in a beautiful pea green boat.

It's nearly seven. If it's going to get light at all today, it should begin to soon. The snow has been piling up at a terrific rate, maybe a foot an hour, and it's getting hard to push the door open. I'm glad I decided to bring all that wood in when I did. At six, I tried to get a weather report, but of course the batteries are dead. Sister Benedict is a flake. I made a pot of coffee. Thank god there's lots of coffee. I don't feel the least bit sleepy. Anyway, I can't imagine going to sleep with that corpse lying on the couch there. Now that day is almost here I'm beginning to worry. Last night with the whole night to get through and this whole story to tell, it was like being in limbo. There wasn't any point in worrying. The way Scheherazade felt, maybe. Well, there's a whole lot of the story to tell, and, the way it looks, a lot more storm to tell it in. Not to worry, Alex! Just carry on. Bulletin: Chester Brown has stopped twitching. The squirrel has stopped sneezing. I can almost imagine it's just another winter day on Monte Cassino. I think I'll imagine that the bundle on the couch is just a month's accumulation of laundry! It's happened before.

After Santa Clara left that day, I took a hike. I walked up

Middle Street, then down to Water street, and pretty soon, as I criss-crossed town, I began to notice the houses and the lighted windows and to become aware of the mystery of all those lives being lived, and bit by bit I calmed down. Along about ten I stopped at Whippers and bought a quart of ice cream thinking maybe there'd be a good movie on cable.

Climbing the stairs to the apartment, I thought I smelled popcorn. Turned out to be my son Scott come to visit.

Scott, then, was twenty-two going on twenty. He was a senior at USM. Jennifer, who was getting her Masters at the University of Texas, was always after him to transfer. She said he was going to wet-brain if he stayed much longer in Maine. I think she exaggerated, but no question, he did drink too much and he smoked too much dope. He seemed straight enough that night. Though underneath the smell of popcorn and yeast, I thought I detected the acrid odor of pot. He offered to share his popcorn with me, and I divvied up the ice cream into two bowls. He was watching E.T..

When the movie was over he asked did I mind if he smoked a joint. I said I did mind, but I wouldn't stop him. He was already rolling one, because that had been my stock reply for years. He said did I know somewhere some people could hide out for a few days. I said, no, I didn't.

He said, "Alex! It's real important. I mean, like they could all get killed."

"Who could all get killed?"

"These people I'm telling you about."

I guess I just assumed he was talking about some friends he was afraid might OD or something. I said I was tired and was going to hit the hay. I said, "How long are you staying?"

"Alex!" he said. "Are you on drugs? I just told you these people need help. I thought...Remember when we were kids one summer you took us to some island off the coast. It had a weird name. I can't remember what they called it."

"Monte Cassino."

"No. That's not it."

"They changed the name. That summer they called it Rerum Novarum. We used to call it 'Rarin' to Go'."

"Yeah! That's it."

"You hung out with Santa Clara and Sister Agnes."

"Santa Clara. Yeah. I remember her. Only you weren't supposed to call her Santa Clara. Sister Clara. That's the place. It'd be perfect. You ever go there?"

"I doubt very much they want to get into drugs."

"Say what?"

"Say what what. Drugs."

"Who said anything about drugs?"

"You did. Didn't you? Someone needs a place to hide out?"

"Yeah. But who said anything about drugs?"

"Scott. I'm really tired. I had a very shitty day and I didn't get any sleep last night. You're welcome to stay. There are flowers in the guest room, a new bed, clean sheets. The whole nine yards. There's even a book of poems on the bedside table. Gerard Manley Hopkins. Sometimes I think he was on drugs."

"I don't know what you're so pissed at. I thought you'd want to help. It's a Salvadoran family. What's left of them. There're five. The mother, her brother, an uncle and two kids. The father was killed plus some others. It's hard to keep straight. They've been working at DeCoster's. There's tons of refugees working at DeCoster's. Did you know that? We're trying to get them across into Canada."

Mother-like I zeroed in. "Who's we?"

"Some of us. Quakers mostly." Scott spent his senior year in Costa Rica on a student exchange program. He speaks Spanish like a native. At least that's how it sounds to me.

I said, "They got you to translate?" He hesitated, took a deep drag on his roach and, holding his breath, nodded. I said, "Tell me the truth."

"That's the truth."

"Yeah but, what else?"

"Look. Forget it." We looked at each other for a while.

I said, "Jen's worried about you."

"Jen's a pain in the butt." He said, as an after thought, "You think she doesn't smoke?" Then he said, "You ever hear of Jim Corbett?"

"No. Should I have?"

"He's been bringing refugees across the border. From El Salvador and Guatemala. A couple months ago, some churches said they were sanctuaries, you know, like in the Middle Ages?—and families are staying in them. You know, out in the open, like defying the INS. Well, Jim Corbett's the guy organized all that.

"But a lot of the families they just kind of want to lay low, you know, get on with their lives. Like they're not real political even if probably they'd of been killed if they hadn't escaped. Besides, there's more of them than churches, so... Anyway, we're helping them cross the border into Canada. It's like during slavery. You know. The Underground Railroad?

"I thought of that island. Like, who'd even know they were there? But I couldn't remember the name. So I thought you'd help."

Let me set the record straight on how I feel about pot. First, some of my best friends turn on. But I'm not there when they do, 'cause I think it's weird what they get like when they're doing it. Spacey. Not there. I hate it when Scott smokes. He thinks I just have a hang-up. That may be. But here he is, looking to me like a young Jewish intellectual, a radical young Jewish intellectual, his hair's very curly and a little on the long side—he looks like my dad, actually—a kind of '80s Abbie Hoffman. But it's like he's lobotomized half the time. And I definitely do not want to screw around with the INS if my partner's suffering from lobotomy, even partial lobotomy. I told him so.

He said, "You're right!"

Now that's a conversation stopper. Before I could think of

a come-back, there was a knock on the door. It was Santa Clara. She had changed into work clothes. You could tell because they smelled of the barn, and other things. Maybe that's why she didn't detect the odor of Scott's pot. But she could see him from the doorway, dimly.

The only light was from the street. After the movie, we had just sat there in the dark talking. It must have seemed to Santa Clara like a den of thieves. Of anarchists plotting. She said, "I'm sorry, you have company, I'll go."

I grabbed her arm as she turned to leave. "It's an old friend of yours," I said. "He's here looking for you as a matter-of-fact."

Scott recognized her right off the bat, but, of course, she had no idea who this guy was turning on in my living room. Scott said, "Excellent! How you been?"

Santa Clara said, "I can't stay."

I turned on the overhead light. Both Santa Clara and Scott let out a howl. Defensively I said, "I thought it might be nice if we could see."

Scott said, "Turn it off. I'll light a candle. Alex, you got any candles?"

Santa Clara had wheeled around and was making for the door. Risking my feet to her steel-toed boots, I put my body in her way. "Hold on," I pleaded. "Don't you recognize Scott?"

Scott, holding a candle, entered the hall from the kitchen. "Sister Clara, don't you remember me? You and me and Sister Agnes, we cleared for pasture out on the island. I was eleven."

Santa Clara stopped pushing me long enough to give Scott a once-over. She looked me in the eye, a glance that gave my heart a workout. "It's your son," she said.

"Yeah. Scott. He came by. He wanted me to get in touch with you." Taking advantage of her divided attention, I nudged Clara back toward the living room, toward one of the chairs. I said, "We ate all the ice cream, but there's popcorn. Would you like some tea? Or some coffee?" Not expecting an answer, I went on to decide. "At this time of night, you probably prefer tea. And with lots of milk. What about you, Scott?"

"Tea's fine by me," said Scott.

"Well, tell Clara your problem," I suggested.

"Are you warm enough?" I asked. Santa Clara looked white and drawn. She was hugging herself like she was freezing. She sat perched on the edge of the chair, her feet off the floor, heels hooked on the rung, eyes downcast.

When I asked was she cold, she jumped, startled, and said, "What?"

"Are you cold? You look uncomfortable."

"No. I'm fine. I should be going."

"Well. Have some tea and hear what Scott has to say. I am going to turn on the heat." And I did.

In the kitchen, I could hear Scott's voice, not what he said, just that he was talking. But before the corn was done popping, I also heard Santa Clara's soft murmur in response. I was some relieved. She would maybe stay.

Then, of course, I began to obsess on the problem of what to do with Scott. Would she stay if Scott stayed? Could I turn Scott out? How could I turn out my own son. It was two in the morning and he had no wheels.

But the world turns, popcorn pops, tea water boils, and in due course I returned to the living room with refreshments. The two of them seemed to have reached some agreement on whatever scheme Scott had proposed to her. They seemed to be ironing out details. Lots and lots of details.

Even with the heat on, it was cold on the floor, which is where I was sitting. There was nothing on TV. And it was going on forty-eight hours since I'd had any sleep. Suddenly I didn't care who slept where or even who stayed. I said, "Hey, you guys, I'm beat. See you in the morning."

Or something like that. If they heard me, they gave no sign.

Chapter Eleven — Gray

In the gray beginning of years...

When I came to, the sun was up and my bed seemed to be occupied by an army. There was this smell, like a blend of diesel fuel and manure and something else, wet feathers maybe, and I was being pushed relentlessly off the edge. I landed on all fours next to Santa Clara's steel-toed boots. She was the only person I could see in the bed. Except for her boots, she was fully clothed right down to her bandanna coif, though it had slipped, revealing her ear nestled invitingly in a soft curl of red hair. But the smell! I decided to go brush my teeth and start the coffee.

Halfway through my second cup, someone ran a bath. Turned out to be Santa Clara not Scott. She came silently, bare-footed, into the kitchen. She takes her coffee black. I poured her a cup. She didn't say anything for a while, just sat there hunched over, holding the mug in both hands, as if they were cold and she needed to warm them. Her wet hair lay fanned over her shoulders, over the blue work shirt fraying at the collar; a hank of her hair caught on a curl of wood-shaving that stuck to some amber pitch.

She wore the same work clothes she wore to bed, but there in the kitchen they didn't smell so bad, just a whiff of the farm. It seemed nice actually, fresh, a kind of out-of-doors smell, better anyway than that fresh air spray they sell. I did make a mental note to change the sheets. I felt too tired still to undertake a conversation, seeing I would probably have to do the talking for the both of us. So we just sat there, sipping coffee, looking out the window and day dreaming.

Sunday morning and it was real quiet out. Funny looking clouds filled the sky. I think it's called a mackerel sky, but I couldn't remember whether that meant it would turn out nice or rotten. Little propeller seeds on the maple had begun to fall, and everything was lacy, delicately colored in pastel shades of green and yellow and rose. When I'm rich and famous, I'm going to travel so that for one whole year I'll be in the middle of that week in spring when everything is on the brink of becoming.

When Santa Clara broke the silence, she said, "I would like you to come live with me. At Monte Cassino."

"What do you mean with you?" I asked without enthusiasm, mistrustful, though too trusting by far considering the kind of spiritual advice she went in for.

"Well," she said, and she raised her head to look me full in the eye for one of those fleeting moments that take in eternity. "I know where I can build us a place easy." Her eyes had a wild gleam I had never seen in them before, but which I was to see often in the years ahead: she got it when she contemplated building. A wag who lived on the island one winter said Santa Clara had an edifice complex. He was right. If Santa Clara wasn't erecting a building, she turned morose.

Her idea was to expand the human side of the barn, that cow stall Jennifer and I had put up nine years before. She wanted me to join her there. It seemed a mixed blessing at best. Notice: I had begun already to take on Santa Clara's habit of understating negatives. Santa Clara had just described how we would turn the chickens out of the barn into an adjoining lean-to, which she intended to let me build, when Scott entered looking frowzy and sullen.

"You drank all the coffee and didn't make more," he

accused.

Santa Clara said, "I have to run."

"Hi, Sister," said Scott. "She wouldn't start?"

"No," said Santa Clara, pulling back her hair and twisting it. "Wouldn't turn over."

"Truck trouble?" I asked.

"Starter," said Santa Clara.

"Let me have my coffee," said Scott. "Alex and I'll give you a push."

The easy rapport Scott and Santa Clara had established ten years before seemed to have resumed. I envied it. She actually talked back to him. Among other things, this gave him space in the conversation to disagree with her.

"You two settle anything last night?" I asked.

She said, "No."

Enthusiastically Scott said, "Wicked right we did." The resuscitating effect of coffee on Scott is amazing.

I said, "I see."

"Tell her, Sister," Scott demanded.

She smiled at him. She said, "We've agreed that if a family needs sanctuary of course they can come to Monte Cassino. We welcome everyone, especially those whose need is greatest. Is that what you mean, Scott?"

"Correct. But that's not all you said."

"Well, we would help to take them across into Canada if they were in danger. Of course we would."

"I see," I said again. "Well, what did you disagree about?"

Santa Clara busied herself tying her head in her bandanna. Scott, too, seemed to have lost interest in the conversation.

"Hello," I said. "Anyone home? Anywhere?" Leaving things in the air like that makes me anxious. The two of them seemed happy as clams. So I asked if they wanted more coffee.

Together they replied, "Thanks, but I've got to hit the road."

Santa Clara's truck seemed to have no trouble starting

and she offered to drop Scott off on the Interstate. I stood on the running board to say good-by. I said in Santa Clara's ear, "About what we were talking about. Before. You know." She kept on looking straight ahead out the windshield. Her wipers, clacking back and forth, made little headway against the grime on the glass. She seemed lost in thought, or lost in space. Lost anyhow. I tried again. "You know, about those renovations to the barn?" She nodded. "Well, I wondered. Do you want to start on those? Like soon?" She kept on nodding. God knows where her mind was. "Clara? What do you think?"

"That's a good idea," she murmured. "A good idea."

"So? When? Will you call me?"

"Sounds good," she said, her head going back forth, mindless as a metronome. "Sounds good."

Scott intervened. "Hey, Alex! It's been great seein' ya. I'll be in touch."

Santa Clara let out the clutch and the truck bucked into gear.

I jumped off. I said, "Yeah." I waved as they rounded the corner of Sewall Street heading off toward the Interstate. There was too much mud on the window for them to see, even if they did happen to look back, either of them. I stood there in the drizzling rain feeling dejected. Twice in twenty-four hours Santa Clara had just up and walked out on me. Did this mean it was true love? You know, not going smoothly and all. When I thought that thought, I thought I thought it ironically.

Chapter Twelve – Turquoise

Turquoise, a fantastic sort of color.

It was a while before any of Scott's refugees came to Monte Cassino either for sanctuary, or as a stopover on the Central American Underground Railroad. And when they did begin to come, they were not from DeCoster's after all. They arrived directly from Harlingen, Texas, where Scott, when he graduated from USM, took a job as a paralegal with Proyecto Libertad. And that's how Mr. Chester Brown, the body on the couch over there, got involved. But I'm getting ahead of my story.

As it turned out life on Monte Cassino with Santa Clara bore a superficial resemblance to Purgatory. Superficial because Purgatory's supposed to be temporary. Monte Cassino, it began to seem toward the end, maybe wasn't. I'll tell some stories from those days, you'll see what I mean.

This storm reminds me of the blizzard of '82, my first winter on the island. It was a northeaster, too. Started on my birthday. Santa Clara and I spent two whole days in bed. Best birthday I ever had in my life, period. And the only one Santa Clara and I celebrated in quite that way. By my next birthday, I had fallen victim to that old 'Sister Benedict Syndrome', which, remember, was the condition, christened by Father Frank, that current favorites of Santa Clara succumb to when her next darling happens upon the scene. Aka jealousy. Very black marking pen reserved for that chapter.

As it turned out, I never got around to making that lean-to for the chickens. They just had to hustle. Get up early on a winter morning and you would see them perched along Jonathan's back for warmth. My 'bedroom,' the former chicken coop, never got finished either, though I did manage to get it pretty well mucked out. Not entirely. But in winter you didn't notice the smell, much, and in summer, you're never indoors except to sleep. Not that I slept there.

Santa Clara did have me set up a bed, that one I got for her in Augusta, the one she never slept in either. And she had me sell my double bed, she said her cot was big enough for us both. It was, too, so long as we both slept on our side and neither of us moved. Those screw-on Hollywood legs would never have taken the weight, especially after my first Black Fast, but the bed's the one Jennifer and I built. Built into the wall, sort of like a bath tub. I know it sounds improbable.

To put the record straight, those two days of my birthday, those two days we spent in bed together, we spent them in the couch there where our friend Chester Brown, if that's his real name, is lying. It opens out. Sister Benedict had gone on retreat for January and February, something she took to doing the year after Beulah, the year Sister Agnes came, the year that Fr. Frank identified and gave a name to the 'Sister Benedict Syndrome.'

"To start the new year on the right foot," Sister Benedict always explained. A bare foot, she might have added, as these retreats of hers happen in Honduras, at a little place her mother has on the Caribbean. While she was away, Santa Clara and I would stay down here in her house, Immaculate Conception, where me and Chester Brown are now as I write.

My last year here, the community was quite small. That summer, only Sisters Benedict and Agnes, Santa Clara and myself lived on the island. But in September, a couple of weeks after school started, a family joined us. They arrived on the mainland shore one evening with nothing but the clothes on their backs and a box of apples they had picked at Newalls Orchard out on the highway. Santa Clara spotted them from the ridge where she was felling trees for winter wood. The tide was in, so they couldn't walk across. She said didn't I think someone should go see what they wanted. It was after five and I was bushed, having spent the afternoon mucking out the barn.

"Alex," said Santa Clara, "some people are over on the mainland standing by the dock. Don't you think someone should go see what they want?"

"I guess so," I admitted, then, compulsively, added, "I guess you think it would be a good idea if I went."

But Clara had drifted away. I ran the pick-up down to the spit and rowed across. The man, his name it turns out was Adam, was short, about my size only skinny, with a scraggly beard and dirty eye-glasses.

He called out to me. "Greetings!" he yelled. "Greetings, Sister." There was an off-shore breeze, it being evening, so I heard him clear as a bell. But I saved my breath til I slipped alongside them at the dock.

"I'm not a Sister," I began. "My name is Alex."

"Sister," he maintained, "I'm Adam and this here's my wife, Eve, and my boys, Cain and Abel. Say hello to Sister," he nudged them.

Eve was a little taller than her husband and, like him, and like the boys, she had long blond hair that was dirty and tangled. Thin and pale, all four seemed under-nourished, their complexion mottled with pimples and scars. The boys and their mother were shy, or intimidated—that thought crossed my mind. Eve bobbed her head in my direction, she kept her eyes fixed on the ground. The boys, who looked to be about eight or nine, hid behind her skirts.

"God sent us," Adam continued in the chatty sort of way

he might have said, "I was born in Chicago."

Non-committal, I replied, "Oh yeah?" I helped them and their box of apples into the boat. The dinghy is small, really only meant for two. We rode back shipping water, exciting the boys to squeaks of pleasure. Adam entertained us with stories of God, or more precisely with his, Adam's, dealings with God. God, he said, had sent them to work with Santa Clara whom he had seen on television. Television, Adam implied, was God's stock medium for communicating with him.

It was clear by the time we reached the island, that God had conferred His blessing on Monte Cassino, and Santa Clara, when He sent Adam and his family to us. Trinity, the three-room building Santa Clara had erected for priests, Mass, and community, had been empty since early spring, so the Adams family (as they quickly came to be referred to) moved right in.

It was ten days or so past Labor Day and the start of school, a time of brilliant days and crisp nights. Cain, the older boy, was, like me, an early riser. The first morning after their arrival, I was out a bit before five. Behind the crenelated silhouette of pointed firs to the east, the sky had begun to thin, a wash of pale lime.

I was thinking about Stupor Mundi, the rooster who through summer had woken and then accompanied me in the pre-dawn rituals of scattering grain to the chickens and hay to Felicia, our Holstein, and Jonathan, Santa Clara's horse. I found Stupor Mundi dead, or nearly so, one morning the end of August. It must have been a terrible fight by the looks of him; but, since none of the hens had been harmed, the other guy's condition must have been even worse.

Stupor was big, and mostly white; the black feathers of his wings and back lay like a tux over the pompous swell of his chest, white as a freshly laundered shirt. He would pace beside me, about two yards off, reserved and judgmental, while I made my rounds, there to see I did things right, and

78

to keep his flock in order. When he died, I expected things to fall apart and was relieved to find that we, the hens and I, could manage on our own without his supervision. But I missed him.

We had worked together, Stupor and I, long enough so that I did not need his crowing in order to wake before dawn. Santa Clara slept on the inside of the cot, her face to the wall, so that I could roll out early and not disturb her. Also, I found that inside position claustrophobic. Santa Clara's back, itself a two foot wall beside me, made me feel, the one time I offered to sleep on the inside, like a character from Dumas, immured.

The morning after the Adams family came, Cain was waiting, as Stupor Mundi once had, on a rock half way between the bedroom door and that part of the barn where Jonathan and the hens hung out. Like Stupor, he followed me on my rounds, silent, judgmental and distant.

When I called out to him in the end, "Well, Stupor, how did I do?" he burst into tears and said, "Everybody calls me stupid." I had my arms around his shoulders trying to explain when Adam caught us.

"He botherin' you, Sister?" Adam bellowed from the doorway of Trinity. The early morning light was soft and golden, the smell of wood smoke elusive in the air. We, Cain and I, had made our rounds in a companionable silence hardly aware that day had broken. Adam's bark startled us awake. Cain wiped his eyes and pulled away from me. "You git in here!" Adam yelled.

I hung onto Cain by his collar. "There's no problem, Adam. We were just feeding the animals."

"You sure, Sister?" he said. "Don't want him botherin' you none."

If I'd've had a clue where it was going to end, right then I would've said, "Nope. Not sure at all. Cain, you git. Like your daddy told you to."

'Cause what happened next is Adam comes sauntering

out of Trinity, his hands in his pockets, his beard a kind of moth eaten stubble, his Dickey pants held up with striped suspenders a good two inches wide over a dingy gray insulated undershirt, on his feet a broken pair of moccasins.

"You're real good with kids, Sister," he said. "I bet you anything you're a teach, knew it I first laid eyes on you I said to myself that Sister likes kids."

How do you say no to a run-on sentence like that? It's like, "Have you stopped beating your wife?" Say "No, not me," and, except for W. C. Fields, everyone's going to think you're a creep.

Adam said, "These boys of mine, they need a teacher. That must be why God brought us here."

I said, "No way," and dropped Cain's neck like it had turned to slime. I gave him a shove down the path toward his father.

But Adam wouldn't let it alone. After dinner that night, Adam and Eve came by the barn. They said...well Adam did the talking. "No way," he said, "are those boys of mine goin' to no public school when they kin get better teachin' right here at home. Besides, this here's a island. How're they gonna git to school in the first place? Huh? Answer me that?"

It got to be a stand-off, Adam and me 'no waying' each other. He wouldn't register them, and I wouldn't teach them. Finally Santa Clara said she was tired and had a headache and if we wanted to keep on arguing, "Maybe you could go to your own room, Alex?" she said.

I was tired too, and in no mood to continue this ridiculous discussion in a dirty chicken coop, so I said, "Well then, I'll take them down to school myself in the morning, and I'll register them."

"Fine and dandy," said Adam, "but tell me this, who do you think's gonna take them to the bus stop every morning and bring 'em back again every night?"

"Don't worry about it," I said. So that's how I got to be Adam's *locum tenens* for Cain and Abel in the school system.

In the school system and generally in the world outside Monte Cassino.

It was clear by their first report card that their previous education hadn't made much of an impression on them. Adam tried to reward their 'Fs' with a belting. After that, I supervised their homework. Cain continued to supervise my morning rounds, *locum tenens* for Stupor, though he never crowed.

It was impossible to work with the boys at Trinity. Adam either made fun of them or would brag to me. Santa Clara was morbidly private and wouldn't let us use 'her' bedroom, so we began to use 'mine.' The boys thought it was a riot, calling a chicken coop my bedroom, and after a while, after they got to know me a little and to trust me some, they started calling me Chicken. Cain, of course, knew I didn't sleep there. But that was our secret. I don't think he ever let on to his folks. Adam, of course, was homophobic, and he continued to call me Sister. And I continued to call Cain Stupor, or Stupor Mundi. Once he knew it meant Wonder of the World and was an Emperor's nickname he loved it. He had me tell him stories about Fred Two and the Crusades, and after I had told him all the stories I knew, I began to make them up.

Around their folks and other adults, Cain and Abel continued to act like mice. Around me they began once in a while to roar. Like I said, in private they called me Chicken. Sometimes all they would say to me, as we sat at our makeshift desk with just a candle or a kerosene lamp to light our work, was "Brk, brk, brk, brk." They'd answer a question with "Brk, brk, brk, brk, brk," and giggle. Next report card they didn't get any As, but no Fs either. And their marks for conduct slipped, which I figured was good too.

During those months when Sister Benedict took her retreat on the Caribbean shore, Santa Clara and I stayed here at Immaculate Conception, and the boys and I faithfully did our homework at the big oak dinner table over there under the gas light. The only interruption in this routine was that northeaster I told you about, the one on my birthday, the one that lasted for two whole days and Santa Clara and I spent all of it in bed together. She was nervous someone would come and find us there, but I said not to worry. I said trust me. I said if someone was dumb enough to come down in that storm, we'd just say we had chicken pox and they best go away again.

"The chicken pox?" she said.

"Why not?"

She couldn't bring herself to say the word 'naked,' as in, 'But we're lying here in bed naked.' Instead she kind of rolled her lovely eyes around in her head and touched the tip of my naked breast with her finger. The light was bad, but I think she blushed.

I spoke to her unasked question. "We can say we have a fever and it got too hot for pajamas." Then I touched her breast and for the longest time she didn't seem to worry about anything.

No one came. Not until after the storm was over. Then who showed up at Monte Cassino but Jaspers. Remember Jaspers? Chesuncook. His mother was a Sephardic Jewess who knew Victor Adler (same last name as mine), and traveled to Mexico with Trotsky (politics similar to mine). Well, back at Chesuncook that's who his mother was.

Jaspers came with someone named Clara. We put her in the little building we call the Tool Shed. And the reason we call it the Tool Shed is we thought if the planning board ever discovers we built it without asking their permission, they won't be so pissed they'll make us tear it down since, after all, it's only a tool shed. That may be crazy. But probably it's not as crazy as calling the chicken coop my bedroom. Or maybe they're equally crazy. After a while at Monte Cassino, degrees of craziness become difficult to distinguish. Jasper's Clara became known as Toolshed Clara. My Clara we took to calling Chainsaw Clara. Some people began to shorten their names to TSC and CSC, but, I noticed, all of them once worked for the government.

Toolshed Clara looked like an idealized version of a grandmother, my idealized version anyway, a Nordic sort of grandmother, built on a heroic scale: you could see her skiing down the mountainside, calm and capable, to warn the village on the fjord of a Nazi plot—or to deliver a baby. She wore her graying hair sometimes in one long braid, but most often in a coronet, adding two inches to an already impressive stature. Her hands matched her build, strong, long-fingered and graceful. She had followed Jaspers to Monte Cassino to serve God and to save money. She needed an operation, they explained. For hours on the night of their arrival we lampooned the medical industry while we sympathized with our new-found friend in Christ, Toolshed Clara, decent, middle-aged, needing medical care she could not afford, an operation, never named, whose precise nature, through delicacy, we carefully avoided learning.

The next evening, Jaspers and Clara came down to have dinner with Clara and me. After the meal, when Cain and Abel showed up to do their homework, the four of us were sitting around the table still, and still attacking the medical industry for its callous disregard of people and the doctors' heartless lack of concern for anything but profit, profit, profit.

Jaspers, early in the evening, let Santa Clara know that his mother was a direct descendant of Pocohontas. Clara, Santa Clara, had said something about being a half-breed. "My mother is a Passamaquoddy, which makes me a half-breed," she pronounced haughtily, with a kind of snobbery, the way she does.

"That's funny you should say that," said Jaspers. "My mother was a direct descendent of Pocohontas. I bet," he said, "we're kissin' cousins." He cackled, his foot whirling loosely on the socket of his ankle.

Santa Clara had broken into the stores for a bottle of Mass wine, which the new Clara, with her elegant, long-fingered hands, took charge of. It was not long before the fifth was gone and another bottle, this time a half-gallon, was dredged from the back of the cupboard beneath the sink.

No homework got done that night. I remember noticing at some point that the boys seemed to have wine, too, but Cain leaned over to reassure me. "It's only grape juice," he whispered. Then he added, "Brk, brk, brk, brk, brk." But in a voice so low that even I could barely hear. I felt vaguely alarmed. Cain's 'brk, brk, brk,' sounded dimly like a threat.

Except for this one aside, neither of the boys said a word. Jaspers, of course, did most of the talking, while the new Clara poured. Santa Clara delivered a brief denunciation of capitalism before she subsided, weary from a day spent wasting the woods.

I said very little for I was obsessed with curiosity: whatever had become of Jasper's Sephardic mother? She who was an intimate of the famous Austrian socialist with the same last name as mine, Victor Adler; the mother who traveled with Trotsky to Mexico. But I was afraid to ask.

Along about nine o'clock—the wine in the jug had fallen below the half-way mark—new Clara began again to recite her grievances against doctors and hospitals. She said, "I need the operation, of course. My whole future, my very life depends on it."

She was quite beautiful there at the table, in the spill of light from the gas lamp, behind her the gathered gloom of the unlit room like a darkened stage, romantic, dramatic. And the wine helped. I was ready to champion her cause, to denounce doctors and hospitals in the press and on TV, to head up a drive to raise the funds. "You can count on us, Clara," I said.

Santa Clara roused herself sufficiently to begin: "My grandmother, who was a Passamaquoddy Indian, raised ten children on welfare."

"Socialized medicine's a dirty word in this country," I muttered at the same time.

"My grandmother had ten children, every one of them at

home. Do you think a doctor would come to her house?" Santa Clara's voice rose at the question which was entirely rhetorical.

I said, "They pay teachers a salary. Why? Because they need workers who can read. But who cares whether workers are healthy?" My question, too, was rhetorical, and I asked it at the same moment Santa Clara asked hers.

Poor Jaspers! His face was a sight to behold. He looked first at Santa Clara, and then he looked at me. A wild gleam lit his eye as he got a drift of my socialist line. I could tell the moment when my name clicked. Bingo! Adler. Jaspers wasn't off his stride a second. Just started his foot whirling counter-clockwise and he said to me, "Did you know Pocohontas gave birth to a child while she was in England?"

I said no. Well, Jaspers said, she did, and then he start-ed in on the wildest genealogy I ever heard. That child of Pocohontas grew up to be a buccaneer. And was captured by a Spanish galleon. In Spain, Jaspers explained, the bucca-neer married the daughter of a famous Cordovan Jew, a Rabbi, a direct descendent of... You got it! The most famous medieval philosopher of them all, Maimonedes. All of this improbable family tree Jaspers rattled off in a moment. They were Sephardic, of course, and the mother I had wondered about all evening, the Russian Jewess friend of Trotsky, lo and behold!, was one and the same as the mother who was a direct descendent of Pocohontas and kissin' kin of Santa Clara, who seemed to have fallen asleep.

Although Jasper's story hadn't been long in telling, new Clara had become restive in the course of it. "I've heard enough of your mother," she said petulantly. Then, reverting to those majestic tones more in keeping with the look of her, she said, "All my life I've worked for Christ, Sister."

Santa Clara was out of it, and I was slowing down. Clara eyed the bottle and, ignoring the rest of us, poured herself some wine. "Now I need this operation," she said, and drank, "and what do I get? I get a run-around. My doctor said I need it. But the surgeon, he says it wouldn't help." She plumped herself up. "And why does he say it won't help?" She looked at Jaspers and me expectantly. Santa Clara was fast asleep.

Dutifully, Jaspers and I chorused, "Money!" But it came out kind of flat.

"Money!" Clara affirmed. "When I got to the hospital, would they admit me?"

"No!" we cried, getting into it a little more.

"No," confirmed Clara. "They would not. And why wouldn't they?"

"Money!" Jaspers and I shouted with renewed enthusiasm. "Money!" The mouse who was learning to roar, Cain, at my side, drank off his grape juice, wiped his mouth on his sleeve, and stood up on his chair. Clara absently topped up his glass with wine before filling her own.

Cain, taking a deep breath, said, "What's your operation for?" sat down, and before I could stop him, downed the wine. Now Clara leaned far across the table, her maternal breasts covering plates, cups and the tablecloth before her. She stuck out her hands, the long and elegant fingers widespread, and she held them to our faces, mine at least, and Cain's. Jaspers she ignored and Santa Clara had begun to snore, something she never does when she sleeps on her side.

"Do you see these?" she asked. I said I did. Cain nodded, a little nervous. "Are these the hands of a concert pianist?" Cain and I risked a quick look at one another. This seemed a question you didn't want to get wrong. But Clara hurried on. "Of course they are. But now look at this." With the thumb and index finger of her left hand she stretched even wider the thumb and index finger of the right. "See?" she trumpeted.

We nodded, Cain and I. "Yes!" we said; and I wondered what.

"No reach!" exclaimed Clara. Clara drew back her hands, then folded her arms. She sighed. Jaspers, taking advantage

86

of Clara's pause, said, "Sister, you ever hear of Averroes?"

"Yeah," I said. "Wasn't he a second cousin of Maimonedes?" Which checked him momentarily. In the second of silence, Cain piped up. "What's the operation for?" he asked again. Out of the mouths of babes. Or, perhaps, in vino veritas. Whatever.

Clara lunged forward, those long-fingered hands of hers spread wide on the table before her. "For my reach!" she shouted, startling Santa Clara out of her doze. "Once I get that operation, I shall become a concert pianist at last!"

"Not many people know it," said Jaspers, "but Averroes had an illegitimate daughter. A Jewess who married...."

CHAPTER THIRTEEN—SILVER

Silver. To reflect on.

That winter, my last on Monte Cassino, the community consisted of Santa Clara and me, the Adams family, Toolshed Clara and Jaspers. Then, when she returned from the Caribbean, tanned and restless, there was Sister Benedict, and we mustn't leave out Sister Agnes, for whom Santa Clara, now Chainsaw Clara, had built a yurt, perhaps to ameliorate the symptoms of the Sister Benedict Syndrome which, I heard later, Sister Agnes had pretty bad and for a long time.

Along toward the end of January, on a Saturday afternoon, our Sheriff drove across the spit at low tide. Everyone but me was out working in the woods. I was mucking out the barn. It was about two in the afternoon when his four-by lumbered to a stop on the ice.

"Hello, Sister," he said.

You may want to know how come everyone is taking me for a nun all of a sudden. It's not that I started to wear a habit, believe me. None of us did. In fact, we looked dressed for combat, guerrilla warfare against the woods. Life in one of Ché Guevarra's Bolivian focos was probably similar to our life on Monte Cassino; no water, no electricity, no help. We wore jeans, flannel work shirts, steel-toed boots. Most Maine women do, of course, except Saturday night, but what with Black Fasts and no baths, we were distinguishable. And that, I think, is why the locals began to call us Sister. I mean, they could have said, 'you there,' but most Mainers are too courteous for that.

Sheriff Lennie Soper, the one who had just driven up in his four-by to where I was struggling to fill some plastic sleds with frozen horse turds and sawdust, was both courteous and kindly. In his mid-forties, he, and his wife, Virgie, kept foster children, having had none of their own. Sometimes they and whatever children were on hand would join us for worship and supper on a Saturday evening. Sometimes Lennie brought someone who was down on their luck and needed a place to stay til they got back on their feet again, got used to sobriety, found a job, returned to a husband who promised not to beat them any more.

"Hello, Sister," said Lennie.

I was feeling particularly Sister-like that afternoon, in the sense that I hadn't bathed in well over a week and my jeans and denim jacket, between sweat, horse shit and straw, could, like bricks, stand upright on their own.

"Lennie," I panted, "how ya doin'?"

"Goo-wud," he said, making two syllables of it, the way they do down here on the coast. "Goo-wud." He scratched his ear and stuff.

"How's Virgie?" I inquired.

"Goo-wud. Eyuh. Goo-wud."

"And the kids? How many you got now?"

"Goo-wud. Goo-wud. Fo-wuh. We're doin' goo-wud. Uh. Sister Clara around?"

It was one of those winter days when the pale blue sky seems infinite, like you could see Valhalla if it were there, and you know it's not cause you can't, and a presentiment of mortality bites, cold and lonely like the winter air. The air so thin and still and cold, each distant sound in precise detail is audible. Listening, we heard the buzz of Santa Clara's saw and up on the ridge, above the black silhouette of the pointed firs, a pale gray column of smoke rose to mark her exact location.

With my chin I pointed toward the smoke. Then I got to laughing. "We don't call her Sister Clara any more," I said.

"Eyuh?" said Lennie encouragingly.

"Chainsaw Clara. We call her Chainsaw Clara." For a moment I thought I might have gone too far. Lèse majesté. Whatever they might say, our neighbors were fond of their celebrity, and the Sopers adored her.

Lennie asked, "How's that?"

"We got another Clara staying here." Too late I saw the pitfall. If I explained the new Clara's name, Toolshed Clara, and to the Sheriff, God knows what trouble we might be in for with the planning board. Quicklike I said, "What can I do for you, Lennie?"

"Oh, not much. This other Clara." He seemed to be scrutinizing the patch on my pocket. It says CALM DOWN CALM DOWN CALM DOWN. "What do you call her?" His gaze shifted to my boots. His head, cocked at an angle, rested lightly on his fist.

"Oh," I laughed. "Ha ha. Nothing."

Just then Clara emerged from the tool shed. From its chimney a spire of black smoke branded the innocent blue of the sky.

Lennie chuckled. "You wouldn't be calling her Toolshed Clara, now, would you?"

"Nah," I said. "You stayin' for supper?"

"Not tonight. What I wanted to ask Sister Clara was if you all had room to keep someone for, oh, say six months."

I told him the retreat house next to the one Jaspers occupied was free. I asked who he had in mind.

"It's a woman down to Windham," he said. Windham. That's the prison outside Portland. Mostly for men. In the late '70s, women, who previously had been incarcerated in a pleasant farmhouse outside Skowhegan, came to be warehoused there instead.

"Oh yeah?" I prodded after a while.

"Mmmmm," Lennie said. He said, looking at the frozen turds on the orange plastic sled at my feet, "You know, come spring, all that stuff melts." There was a gleam of humor in his eye.

"I'll be damned," I said. "What's her name?"

"Iris."

"She's got no family?"

"She's got a mother. Down to Bath. Doesn't want her. Hard. She had somewheres to go, they'd release her." He looked me briefly in the eye.

"Send her," I said.

He nodded. "Saturday?" climbing back in the cab of his truck.

"No problem."

He turned the four-by around. He slowed as he passed by, touching his orange stocking cap in a salute by way of goodbye.

"It melts in the spring, hunh?" I threw at him.

"You betcha."

"When's that? July? Barn roof's not high enough. By July, the horses couldn't get in the door."

"They don't need no barn after round the first of April. Most years."

After supper that night I told everyone about Lennie's visit. They were all gung-ho, feeling good after the labor of the day, warm and well-fed—more about that in a minute—and charitable in Christ, or something like that. We all agreed Iris could come and I was volunteered to go and fetch her.

About being well fed. The two Claras, it turned out, had more in common than their name. It's not that they cooked alike. They didn't. For instance, Santa Clara really likes red meat, though by the time she's done with it, it's more apt to be black, or even green; whereas Toolshed Clara thinks eating any meat is gross. Chances were, whatever Santa Clara brought to supper would get fed next day to the chickens. Chickens or compost, I decided which. Toolshed Clara's contribution to dinner that first Saturday, however, was in a category by itself. It was black, and it was gooey, and it was unidentifiable. The odor was, to be kind, pungent. Bad as it was, though, it was better than what she brought the following week which was just the same only more so.

"Good God!" said Adam when he took off the lid. "What in hell is this?"

"Your language, like your metaphor," said Clara with withering condescension, "is lacking in imagination as well as taste."

"Say what?" Adam replied, helping himself to the chicken stew Eve had made. He didn't waste a glance on Santa Clara's casserole, which, though it looked like layered cardboard, was really stuffed cabbage. I know. I saw it before it began to cook. And cook. And cook.

The secret of the Claras' culinary art was time. Maybe even patience. This was especially true of Toolshed Clara. Santa Clara's dishes perhaps owed more to absent-mindedness than to patience. Absent-mindedness on Santa Clara's scale, however—for instance letting this cabbage casserole cook overnight in a 300 degree oven—was almost an art form. Or her rescue attempts were. This particular dish she rehydrated after breakfast with a dollop of water from the spring, over-doing it of course, so that she was forced to dry it out again with another nice warm bake in the oven. "It's good food," she always assures us when she uncovers each week's masterpiece. But not even she would call it gourmet fare.

Toolshed Clara was less reserved. "Of course it's gourmet," she said of her mess. "Though that is hardly the issue. Yeast!" she proclaimed. "Yeast!" With the extra two inches gained by her coronet of braids, Toolshed Clara towered above us all. Her clarity of diction, her regal poise made it easy to snigger, and hard sometimes to keep a straight face. "Yeast," she said, "is everywhere."

While we did our best to look serious, Toolshed Clara opened up her mouth and through the yawning gap inhaled a bushel or so of air. The air, she explained, was laden with spores of yeast. "Bs!" she trumpeted. "Bs!" At first I thought she said bees. "Vitamins," Clara clarified. "B vitamins."

She brought her mess to supper in a little aluminum pan, veteran of many fires, crusted and black. In it she had, over the years, collected unimaginable thousands, perhaps millions, of yeast spores. She gathered them on the accumulated refuse of each day's meals: her breakfast oatmeal, supper's rice, crusts of bread, remnants of fruits and vegetables both raw and cooked. Each Wednesday and Saturday, these collector's items were Toolshed Clara's contribution to our community supper. In reply to Sister Agnes's exclamation of disgust, Toolshed Clara, disdainful sure, but with a measure of noblesse oblige, explained, "Yeast kills bacteria, of course." She smiled loftily. "That's the whole point. Besides, it's only vegetable matter. NOT dead animals." She glared down at Santa Clara who, except for her body, wasn't there anyway.

Adam said, catching on, "Oh yeah. Like penicillin."

Clara smirked modestly. I noticed, though, that Adam didn't eat any. In fact none of us, except for the Claras, did, even though, color-wise, it was perfect for our Black Fast which, of course, is supposed to go on until Easter. Clara took all that was left home with her, the better to collect more spores, so I didn't have to choose between the chickens and the compost to dispose of the remains.

That evening's pièce de résistance was Eve's chicken stew, coq-au-vin really—you could taste the wine. It surprised me because the Adams had no money and, where it was going into the last of the month, I knew they were out of food stamps. Between the stew, my salad, and a loaf of bread Jaspers brought, we managed all right. And the chickens next day approved Santa Clara's reconstituted cabbage casserole, though there was more of it than they could handle. There seemed to be only nine of them left.

When I first came to the island, there were thirteen hens and Stupor Mundi. While the hens and I bumped along mornings okay without Stupor, and what with Cain to help me I didn't even miss him so much any more, every so often since fall, ever since Stupor died, ever since the Adams family came to Monte Cassino to live, we lost a chicken to a fox. Saturday mornings sometimes I'd come out and I'd find chicken feathers lying all around. You could see there'd been a struggle. But never a sign of the hen. She'd just been carted off, I supposed, by the fox to his lair. That Saturday before Iris came, we were down to nine.

The trip to Windham from Monte Cassino is a good hundred fifty miles. The vehicle I had to make it in was a little brown Datsun pick-up truck 'donated' to the retreat (abandoned at the spit) and which, if you had any trouble with the engine stalling (if!), all you had to do was stick your feet through convenient holes in the floorboard and push. The door on the passenger side Santa Clara tied up fresh that morning with new plastic clothesline that wears like iron, and everyone chipped in for gas and the eight quarts of oil we figured it would take to get there and back. The carburetor was beyond repair, so the holes in the floor were convenient for those in-town traffic situations when the engine stalled, which it always seemed to do at the worst possible time. But out on the highway, so Santa Clara said, she was 'good transportation.' Maybe. She had a wicked shimmy at fifty, so you had to decide whether to go at forty or sixty, knowing you were better off at forty, but dying to get the whole thing over with.

I made it to Windham in four hours on three quarts of oil. By-passing Augusta, I stalled out only once where it was really dangerous; and then the engine caught first try, so I sailed out from under a pulp truck coming along Route 202 there outside Gardiner. That sucker had a ten-ton load and was doing fifty easy. He sat on his horn instead of his brakes, and I thought for sure it was trumpets I was hearing. The ones they blow at the pearly gates.

Whatever that little Datsun lacked in the way of mechanical devices—stuff like carburetor, valves, muffler, brakes—she made up for in spiritual aids. Saint Christopher smiled from the dash, and suspended from the sunshade were a Miraculous Medal, a Scapula, and a string of worry beads. Someone had wired a Palm Sunday frond, dried beyond recognition, to the overhead light. I decided, as a token of my gratitude for escaping the pulp truck, to add to this collection. I thought about getting St. Jude, champion of lost causes, to travel there beside St. Christopher. Until someone hit the lottery, it was probably the most anyone could do for that little pick-up.

Iris, I decided when I met her, was rather sweet, but if she was glad to see me, she didn't give herself away. I realized later she was probably just dazed seeing me climb out the window then top up the engine with three quarts of oil. Iris is kind of the opposite of Toolshed Clara. She's a sort of ersatz Dolly Parton, but without the glitz, and, that day, without the bounce. Her hair was badly bleached, and much too often. But you could tell what she was driving at with her high-heeled boots and fish-net stockings, the blouse with little plastic in-laid buttons and buckskin-like trim. For luggage she had a cardboard box with the top flaps folded so they stayed shut. We were standing in the little reception room.

"Hold on," I said. "Stay here while I stow this for you." I sort of secured her box by laying the spare tire on it, that and the lug wrench, and then I covered it all with a tarp because it was beginning to look like snow. Before I went back for her, I thought to untie her door, I wasn't sure she would fit through the window, plus it would have been awkward. I saw her smile at me through the picture window. It made me think she might be sweet. That and grateful. See, the others never saw her smile at all, which is why, probably, they always spoke of her as that ungrateful woman from the prison, what's her name.

Her story was sad. Talk about being more sinned against than sinning. Growing up in Bath, pretty much on the street, pretty much on her own, she got arrested often, for stealing mostly, food and stuff she really needed, and then, later on, for soliciting. She made her way down to Portland when she was about twelve. When she got a little older she worked for a while at the Parisienne Massage Parlor there on Congress Street, having apprenticed with other teeny boppers across the way at the Dunkin Donuts that once stood on the corner. She spent her nights under the portico of the Portland Museum of Fine Arts, and, in winter, in a culvert where they were building a by-pass to enhance the tourist flow. But what happened to get her sent to Windham she said, was not her fault. It was her temper.

We were plugging right along there in Windsor, outside the fairgrounds, when she told me the story. "We was bein' picked up all the time. You know. Sure they put me in foster homes. But they was awful. I mean, like if I wanted a mom, you know, I gotta mom. Hey, she'd do anything to get me back with her. It's not like I need a mom."

"So what happened?" I said.

"I just got fuckin' sick and tired a bein' picked up all the time, you know?"

"Yeah?"

"Yeah. So I slugged this cock sucker. You know. I said to him, I said you keep your fuckin' hands offna me. I said, I ain't goin with you guys no more. So just leave me the fuck alone, I told him. It was like, you know, entrapment. Yeah, entrapment."

"Entrapment?"

"Yeah, entrapment. 'Cause it's like, you know, like with boxers. Like, if they hit someone? You know what I mean. Like in a fight. It's not like with you and me. You know, with a boxer they say he used a deadly weapon. Like what they mean's his fists, where he's a boxer, you know what I mean? So, it's the same thing," she explained

"Oh," I responded. I said, "I see," which was more like a metaphor really than a lie.

"'Cause it's not like those fuckers didn't know I had a temper. You know what I mean?"

I was beginning to. "Like if he messed with you," I ventured, "he'd get what was coming?"

"Bet on it," Iris assured me. "I got some wicked temper." It seemed to please her.

"So," I said after a while, "what happened?"

"Well, this prick he keeps on at me and I said to him, I said, 'Hey, man, lay the fuck off,' so it's not like he didn't know."

"So you figure he, uh, he entrapped you."

"Fucking right he did. Ass-hole." She snorted, two little puffs through her nostrils, and said, "I knocked him out. Funny! Lord, I thought I'd die laughin'."

I said, "Ah!" But I said it cogently, and I carefully stored away the information.

Let me tell you what it looked like to me, our little island, when Iris and I arrived at the spit that Saturday afternoon. It looked like peace. The pointed firs, somber guards, staunch and black, girding the coast, indomitable as parents to a child. The spit itself, a drawbridge, intermittent link to a troubled world, so that at times, magically, our island was a universe unto itself, free of troubles, a refuge where no harm could come.

"What the fuck is this?" Iris cried as I headed down the bank to the spit. She grabbed the wheel. "Where're you takin me? No one said this fuckin' place's an island. What happens when the tide comes in? You ain't takin me on no fuckin' island."

But, of course, her door was tied shut, and there was no way she could climb through my window even if she managed to squeeze across my lap. Up there in the cab, even if she did throw a punch at me, I reasoned, she wouldn't get any power behind it. No room. So I kind of ignored the fact that we were both driving and she had me in a hammer lock. We just moseyed along together to the barn.

"You'll love it," I kept saying. "Trust me." And I kept thinking about the asshole who had entrapped her. I wanted her to calm down some before she got her legs under her and some room to throw a punch.

Now to me, our little community also looked pretty like a picture. A little like, well not Currier and Ives exactly. Turn of the century, yes, but more Grandma Moses, maybe. I didn't see the tattered tar paper; I only saw where we had started shingling with cedar shakes. And to me, they had come to appear reasonably straight. I saw pasture, though I knew perfectly well all that lay behind the broken fencing were boulders, some big enough to rise naked above the snow, five feet deep, or more, on the ground. Jonathan, Felicia and the eight hens (right! Eight. That morning there were only eight and that pitiful little pile of feathers and down), they looked to me like livestock. I didn't even see the three out-houses any more, I had come so much to take them for granted; besides, two of them were roofed. I guess the place had become home.

Iris flatly refused to get out of the truck. "Take me back," she said.

"To prison?" we all chorused.

She elucidated: "Back. I said back. I'm not kidding. I'm telling you. Take me the fuck back. Now!"

I think entrapment's a terrible crime. But compared to turning around and heading right back to Windham, let me tell you, I was tempted. "Could we have supper first?" I asked.

In the end she agreed and let go of my neck. Santa Clara untied her door and Sister Agnes rolled a boulder over for her to step down on. It was all done so graciously Iris said she'd even think about staying overnight and letting us drive her back in the morning but we better not get any ideas. We sailed through the worship service without a hitch.

Sheriff Lennie Soper was there, in civies, and Virgie and a couple of their kids. They had left their car on the other side, of course. Our trouble didn't start until supper. When Iris saw the yeast spores, cleverly disguised as botulism cultures, she said, "Get me outta here!"

Later, Toolshed Clara explained what happened this way. "I only laid a restraining hand on the young lady's arm so that I could explain to her about the Bs."

"Bees," was all Clara had a chance to say. Iris pasted her one with a right to the jaw. Clara's mistake, I guess, was selecting the wrong arm to put her restraining hand on. As you can imagine, all was pandemonium for quite a while, until Clara came around and everyone stopped screaming.

Iris, though, remained calm through it all, above the din of battle, so to speak. Her only contribution, but repeated often, was, "I wanna get outta here. You know? I mean, get me outta here."

The Sopers agreed to drive her back. They left without eating. Not even the Adams' contribution to supper—it was another wonderful coq-au-vin—tempted Iris to stay on at Monte Cassino: "In this fuckin' mad house? No way! Not me! Not one more fuckin' minute!" And she balled her fist, you know, like to make it clear, she wanted outta there.

Chapter Fourteen—Green Again

But as in 'a green and yellow melancholy' green.

Reminiscing about those Monte Cassino days made me clean forget about Mr. Chester Brown over there. Not that I believe for one minute that his name is really Chester Brown. But there's plenty of time to tell about him. This storm's still got a way to blow by the look of things. So long as I have something to write about, I feel okay. And telling stories about those days on Monte Cassino is good for me I think. At the time, none of it seemed funny.

What I can't understand, though, is how come Chester Brown is here on Monte Cassino. If the raid took place, why was he alone? If he wasn't alone, why was he left here? Where was his car? Did I miss it in the storm? Another thing. Maria must have said a hundred times she was afraid Rollie was going to kill Chester Brown... But there I go again, getting ahead of myself.

Thinking about Rollie reminds me of that squirrel upstairs. The one with asthma? I got to wondering whether it was Rollie. I decided if it were, I was better off pretending I hadn't heard him. You don't want to mess around with that dude. Then, about an hour ago, there was a lull in the wind. I went to the outhouse. Since I got back I haven't heard a sound from up there. If it was a squirrel, it's gone off to be with its family. If it was Rollie, god knows where he went. One of the other buildings. Actually, I miss the company!

In the category of stupid thoughts: What if it was Santa Clara I heard upstairs???

It's nearly noon. I've been here what, going on twenty hours. My appetite's come back. I think what I'll do is make myself a baked bean sandwich, like they do in Ireland, then back to life with Santa Clara.

Toolshed Clara's yeast spores kept getting us into trouble right up to the day she left. January thaw set in early that year with a warm wind blowing straight up from Honduras, sent, Sister Benedict implied, by herself. She wrote to us on little picture postcards of quaint native women, hollow-backed by malnutrition. "I'm always thinking of you and remembering you in my prayers. I've asked God to bless you with warm weather."

After the disaster with Iris, things held pretty steady on the farm for a time. We even managed to avoid Sheriff Lennie Soper's next well-meant calamity.

Each low tide, Toolshed Clara and Jaspers trucked across to the mainland so that Clara could call her doctors. Each evening, in the most precise detail, she would construct for us the newest barricade an uncaring Hippocrates had erected to block her road to fame and fortune as a concert pianist. These stories she told a cappella, in the sense she no longer had a chorus to accompany her. When she drew herself up tall and in rolling tones asked "Why?" she had to supply the answer herself.

The children knuckled down to their homework and started to memorize their multiplication tables. This was a triumph for me. At least that's how I thought of it. Adam said it was a victory for Christ. Not that anyone was keeping score; besides, would I grudge Jesus points? What happened is Cain and Abel said no one else in school had to learn the tables so why should they.

"How's that?" I said. "They all going barefoot?" That was a joke, but like Clara, if I wanted a laugh I had to provide it. "Ha, ha, ha," I said. "That was a joke. Bare foot? They could count their toes?" Polite, they smirked.

Cain said, "Sister, all the kids've got computers. You know, the pocket kind. Abel and I, we both want one."

"Each wants one," I counseled absent-mindedly as I thought up some arguments to support my 'no.' "Look," I said, "What if the two of you, say, were out in the woods. Yeah, cutting a cord of wood, and so you cut down a tree and you four-foot it, and you count the pieces. Then Cain says, 'Hey, Abel, this is a big waste of time cutting together. You go cut your share over to Soper's Ridge.' And Abel says, 'Ok. But what is my share?'

"Now," I said, "what are you going to tell him? There you are, out in the woods. No computer. You never bothered to learn your multiplication tables. What are you going to do?"

"Take off our shoes," they said together, neither of them cracking a smile.

"Wise ass," I observed.

Why it was a victory for Christ, according to Adam, when they finally got down to brass tacks and started to memorize those tables (two times two, two times three, two times four, etc., etc.), rather than a triumph for me, is this: I tried a few more clever and imaginative arguments to convince the boys they should learn to multiply, each argument about as effective as that one involving the cord of wood, until finally I decided to price pocket calculators at Zayres and Ames.

This was back before they started giving them away at banks. Those two calculators were going to set me back by as much as my weekly contribution to the community for food. I mentioned this after supper Wednesday night and in no time time flat we had an impromptu antiphon in progress there at Trinity.

Chainsaw Clara: Did you ever hear of anything so outrageous?

Everyone: No!

Toolshed Clara: But then, what is the only thing people care about any more?

Everyone: Money!

Jaspers: Yeah, money.

Everyone: Just money.

Alex: When I was young...

Everyone: We had to learn to multiply.

Claras (together): Now all it is is...

Everyone: Money, money, money.

This was the basic theme. There were variations.

Adam said, "Gee whiz. I was just reading in *Church World* where the Diocese is raising money for St. Andre's up there to Bangor, that home for unwed mothers, like I guess they could use twenty-five dollars better'n you two don't need no computers just set your butts down and put your mind to it."

Everyone: That's right.

But you've probably got the idea by now. So. I don't know what Adam said, or threatened, to Cain and Abel, but the next night when they came down to do their homework, they announced that they had seen the light, they would memorize their multiplication tables, and father (small 'f', they meant Adam) would take care of the donation, I could put my twenty-five dollars in the envelope provided. They handed me the envelope.

Now maybe you're thinking, "That sounds like a victory for Christ why doesn't she let it go." And maybe you're right, except, the boys weren't learning anything. They continued to fail their math, and if I didn't get things on a better track, Adam told me, he was taking the boys out of school. In case you think that was no concern of mine: "Sister," said Adam at breakfast that Monday morning, (winter had kicked back in with a vengeance, sub-zero temperatures and six inches of new snow), "No way am I sending those two sons of mine, in this weather, to that school to be humiliated. No way. If they can't get decent grades in math, you're just going to have to tutor them at home."

This wasn't rhetoric either. I could tell. He didn't expect anyone to answer him back. And no one did, me included.

We had taken to eating breakfasts together these winter mornings. It started on Epiphany when Santa Clara and I invited everyone down to Immaculate Conception for her famous soda biscuits, a recipe her grandmother used to use. So long as she keeps the flour and the soda straight, they aren't half bad. We won't talk about those times Santa Clara gets confused, two cups of soda for two tablespoons of flour. Both being white, it's a mistake, she says, anyone can make. Yeah, anyone who's not all there.

Toolshed Clara, of course, would bring her pet spores, and I'd boil up a pot of oatmeal. If anyone had any left-over Entemann's coffee cake, they'd bring that and we praised the Lord with extra fervor. Sister Agnes brought whatever spoiled fruit she had on hand. As a matter of fact, those breakfasts quickly evolved into occasions for recycling. Some stuff we ate, some was passed on to the chickens, and some went directly into the cycle of compost to garden to summer vegetables to spoiled vegetables to compost again.

This one Monday morning, the morning when Adam spelled out the consequences to me if his boys didn't learn to multiply, Sister Agnes brought us 'the most wonderful sour dough pancake starter in the world.' It came, she said, from Soviet Armenia. By the looks of it, it came steerage. In a crusted little aluminum pot, the starter was black and gooey and it kept going 'plop' all through worship service. Well, I cooked up the pancakes, but no one ate them, except Cain and Abel who said 'Yuck!' and tried to get away with something, again.

Adam explained. "You two're trying to get away with something again. Now you took that, no one made you, and you are going to eat every last bite of it."

Every last bite included a pint of maple syrup and somehow they managed. The rest I threw to the chickens on my way out. Mornings I always took the boys to the bus stop, driving when I could, otherwise rowing. 'And in the afternoon I rowed or drove them back again. That's right, Adam had told me, "If you are so convinced the boys are better off in school than bein' taught at home, well then you know who can take them to the #$%&* bus stop."

That Monday morning I took them clear into school. I had urgent business in town. All my savings had gone to St. Andre's home for unwed mothers, but I needed to get something to raise those boys' math scores. If not pocket calculators, at least flash cards. I told them I would meet them at the spit at four o'clock.

You wouldn't believe how much flashcards cost or how hard they are to find these days. Several clerks suggested I might want to buy a little pocket calculator, and I managed, every time, not to suggest what they might like to do with their suggestion. Finally, in a dusty little bookstore on a side street I found what I was looking for. I got two sets. Altogether, so far, multiplication had set me back thirty-four dollars and change. I tried not to dwell on the two-for-one sale on calculators at Zayre's that day. Two for just twelve ninety-nine. It was a rebate sale. I tried to cheer myself up, reflecting I would have lost my sales slip and never got my money back anyway.

I had to row home. January and February are hard months to get on and off the island because of ice. Some years it gets so you can walk back and forth all the time. But that Monday, after the thaw, it was treacherous. I got back to Monte Cassino a little after noon. Santa Clara was sitting at the big oak dinner table eating pop corn with soy and yeast. Nutritional yeast, the kind you buy in a health food store.

"Want some?" she asked. "I made plenty and there's coffee. It's good food," she added absently, arousing my suspicions.

"Talking about good food," I said. "Could you believe that

Armenian glop Agnes brought to breakfast?"

"Isn't she generous," said Santa Clara.

"Generous? You call that generous?"

"It had been in her family for years."

In her family? Maybe that explained it. "Oh," I said, "I thought it was only a sour dough starter...What's that?" I asked. A letter, several pages thick, scrawled in pencil on yellow foolscap, lay open on the table.

"Lennie Soper was here," said Clara.

"An errand of mercy? It's someone else's turn to go to Windham."

"It's someone in the county jail."

"Oh? What's he in for?"

You might think it showed hardness in me to ask. But when we started taking in prisoners, we agreed no rapists, no murderers, and no arsonists. Of course, our first prisoner had murdered her husband. But that, we decided, didn't count. I mean, when she got here, her jaw was still wired where he had broken it. The two broken ribs and clavicle were mostly healed and didn't show, but we decided to make an exception to our rule anyway.

Santa Clara had a far-away look in her eye. "Hello?" I said. "What's he in for?"

"Alex!" she said, and sighed. Meaning: Alex, why ever are you so hard?

"I want to know."

She handed me the letter.

"You want me to read this?" I asked. "Didn't you read it? What does it say?"

More sighing, so I picked it up. *Dir sista yu or gad wimin lik mi muter tat me wrespek wimin lik u nons. That was the first page*. The second page— *In kris I PRA 4 u in Kris*. There were six pages more. Reading the first two took me about ten minutes. I think the gist of it was that his mother had taught him to respect women in general and nuns in particular and that he prayed to find peace with us here at Monte Cassino.

I laid the letter down. "So you think we should let him come?"

"Poor man," said Santa Clara. "You can see he has been touched by God."

"Touched anyway," I joked, and leaned over to kiss her ear. The sweetest curl of wood shaving dangled from it. My lips were puckered and half way there when Sister Agnes's head appeared before me. Not her body, just her head, and her eyes not two feet from my own.

I froze in mid-pucker. Then I realized she must be looking around the edge of the door having opened it so silently neither Santa Clara nor I had heard her. Caught in flagrante, I made the best I could of my pucker and said 'tsk tsk tsk' in a puckery sort of way, not realizing quite how close I was to Santa Clara's ear. She jumped a foot off her seat banging my nose which started to bleed.

"Knock! Knock!" Sister Agnes warbled, knocking the inside of the door. "Did I startle you? I hope I didn't startle you."

"When I told you to knock," I said, trying to stem the flow of blood with my sleeve, "what I had in mind was you knock before you come in. *Not afterwards!*" And if I'd told her once I'd told her this a million times. Santa Clara glared at me.

Sister Agnes only laughed. "Look!" Sister Agnes exclaimed, "what I brought for you. Some lovely squash!" With the toe of her boot, she shoved a peck of rotten squash across the threshold.

"Oh," said Santa Clara, "what good food!"

I said, "It's rotten."

"It's good food," said Santa Clara, repeating herself.

Sister Agnes said, "Just cut out the bad spots and cook the rest. What you don't use right away, you can freeze."

"I think you're wrong," I said to Santa Clara, ignoring Agnes. "It's not good, it's rotten."

Santa Clara bowed her head and sighed. You could see I was getting to be a pain in the ass. To her. Sister Agnes seemed to find me amusing. She was still just a head in the doorway, and the temperature in the room was falling fast.

"Could you shut that goddamn door?" I inquired. My nose was still bleeding. I guess that's why I felt spleeny.

Santa Clara said to me, "Alex, please don't use that kind of language. Would you hand me a paper towel? You've bled on me." I got two. One for myself. While I fetched them, Sister Agnes took my seat.

"What's this ?" she said, pointing to the letter.

"Poor man," said Santa Clara. "Lennie's made arrangements for him to come to us."

Sister Agnes made soothing noises in the back of her throat.

"Since when?" I said. "You mean you already told Lennie to bring him? Without discussing it with anyone? I live here too!"

"Nothing's been settled," said Santa Clara.

"Poor man," Sister Agnes contributed.

"About this squash," I attacked, from the flank.

"Agnes, yes, thank you for the good food." That was Santa Clara, of course.

"Oh, it's nothing," Sister Agnes assured her.

"What I was gonna say is," I said, "so long as there's this Black Fast, I'll just cook up this squash the way it is, rotten spots and all, then I'll moosh it all together. That way we won't need to use so much molasses to color it."

But they were already talking about something else in earnest, girlish whispers and if they heard me they didn't let on. So I went upstairs to change my shirt. When I came down, Santa Clara was still there, but Agnes had gone.

"About that squash," said I.

"Won't you let it alone?" said the Saint-about-to-undergo-martyrdom.

"Yeah. That's what I was thinking. What I was thinking was where you look on it as good food and real generous of Agnes and all, and you don't like my suggestion for how to fix it, my idea is you fix it. However you want." What could she

108

say? I had the forethought to take a look at her mole, and I did not like what I saw. "See ya later alligator," I said and beat it out of there.

On my way past the barn, I noticed a chicken lying on the snow, kind of like a cat on the grass in the sun, warm and cuddly, and it took a moment for me to realize I'd never seen a hen lying down like that in the snow before. I set her back on her feet. She took a couple woozy steps and then fell over on her side again. Just like a drunk I thought. Funny. I noticed beside her the remnants of Sister Agnes's Armenian sour dough pancakes. The same as Cain and Abel had eaten every last bite of with a pint of maple syrup for breakfast that morning. An uneasy thought began to stir.

"Sister! Sister!" Clara, like a wild woman, burst from the tool shed, Jasper, also agitated, right behind her. "Sister! Sister!"

Such carrying on. I had never seen Clara anything but regal before. I abandoned the chicken to her hangover and went to see what the matter was.

"Sister!" Toolshed Clara caught hold of my shoulders and shook. My teeth rattled like castanets and little red drops of my blood appeared in a spray across her shirt front.

"Let me down!" I suggested.

"What did you do with my spores?" Clara countered, swinging me around some before dropping me.

Jaspers was shouting too. "What did you do with Clara's spores?" he kept asking.

"What did I did with her spores? I didn't do anything with her fucking spores," I said, forgetting myself completely.

"You've got blood all over Clara," Jaspers accused.

"Just her collar. Do you have a tissue?" He did. He handed it to Clara, which was okay; it was dirty anyway. I used my sleeve again.

Toolshed Clara, having let me go, began to wring her lovely, long-fingered hands. "What I brought back from breakfast was that filthy Armenian starter of Sister Agnes's," she wailed.

That's not possible I thought. I said, "You couldn't have. I used up all the starter making the pancakes." Then, "Or at least I thought... "

"You thought!" Clara said savagely, reaching again for my shoulders. I backed up. The uneasy thought that had stirred before, now sat up and stretched. I glanced over to the chicken struggling, like a drunk, to her feet, claws slipping and sliding on the ice. "You deliberately cooked my yeast spores," Clara menaced. Then she wailed, "Do you know what that means?" She began to wring her hands again. Wailing and wringing, she told the world, "You killed my spores. You killed all my spores!"

Alex Adler, mass murderer. I looked at the chicken. I thought: Alex Adler, child poisoner. "Look," I said, "I gotta get to the school."

"What about my spores?"

"What's wrong with Armenian spores?" I asked.

"Sister," said Jaspers, "you know William Saroyan?"

"William Saroyan your mother's cousin?" I threw over my shoulder as I made off down the road to the spit.

They were waiting for me at the school. They had the children lying down in the office. Which was something of a relief. I mean, they weren't dead or in the hospital. Mrs. Grater, the principal, is built, like Toolshed Clara, on an impressive scale. She seemed when she saw me to get all agitated. I resolved whatever happened to keep her at a distance; my nose had taken enough punishment for one day.

"Sister, we can't have this," is how she began. "We must be able to reach you in an emergency. If we can't get in touch with you, then these children can no longer be enrolled in this school."

"How are they?" I asked.

"Oh, they'll recover. But how could you allow it to happen?"

"It was just a mix-up. I didn't do it on purpose," I said

with feeling. The thought of deliberately giving someone those revolting spores disgusted me.

"Well, I should hope not!" Mrs. Grater drew a deep breath, her diaphragm expanding, her bosom billowing. "But I am quite sure it has happened before. Though never so blatantly as today!"

"Oh no! Oh no!" I said. "It never happened before. Clara always takes all of it. No one else ever takes any. Honest to god. She must be used to it, it never seems to bother her."

"Sister Clara?" Mrs. Grater's eyes bugged in astonishment.

"Not Sister Clara," I said. "Toolshed."

"Tool shed"?

"Clara."

Mrs. Grater stepped back a pace. She drew herself even more rigidly erect. Then in withering tones she enunciated, "And I thought you were a Christian community!"

"We are a Christian community," I reassured her, deciding this was not the time to explain that I consider myself an atheist. "You see, I thought it was the Armenian culture."

Her brows gathered in a speculative little frown. Her eyes bored into me. She took a cautious step in my direction. She sniffed. I backed up. "We don't pander to xenophobia in this school!" Mrs. Grater provided this non sequitur in an absent minded sort of way as she took another step toward me and sniffed again.

"Oh good," I said, backing up. "That's good. You shouldn't." Getting back to the matter in hand, I explained, "You see, Sister Agnes brought it. She thought it would be good to have for breakfast."

"For breakfast! Well, I never! For breakfast! Let me assure you, Sister, that is not Armenian. My mother was Armenian." She and Jaspers should get acquainted.

"Well," I said, "I didn't think it looked right, but Sister Agnes did say it was Armenian."

"Well then, someone should sit down and have a talk

with Sister Agnes." This whole time she kept moving in on me, taking these little steps and sniffing. Step, sniff; step, sniff. And I kept backing up.

"Would you mention rotten vegetables? When you talk with her? I mean, she could take them to the compost easy as me," I said, babbling because she was making me nervous.

"What did you say?"

"Rotten vegetables." I had backed slap up against the file cabinet and she was still coming at me, her nose going in and out, sniff sniff sniff, like you do trying to find what's rotten in the fridge.

"Snf, snf. What's wrong with your nose?" she said, her face about a foot from mine.

"Sister Agnes," I promptly accused, wondering what was wrong with hers.

"Sister, have you been drinking too?"

"Nooo! Whadda ya mean, too?"

"The children brought wine—cheap wine—disguised as grape juice, to school. And, they offered it to the other children!"

I started to laugh. Sheer relief. "You mean they're okay?"

"If you call being drunk okay."

"Well, no, but, I thought they might have botulism."

"I have a good mind," said Mrs. G., "to suspend them."

"Oh, Mrs. Grater, don't say that!"

"Well, I am prepared to give them one more chance." She waggled her finger at me again. "One more. But you have to get a CB out there on the island. By Friday."

Staggered, I said, "Do you know what a CB costs?"

"No," she assured me, "I don't. And what's more, I don't care. No CB, no school. And that's final."

I had to give Mrs. Grater credit for one thing: When it came to Christian charity, that woman didn't have a milligram in her whole body.

Cain and Abel coming home were in the repentant stage

of their hangover. I felt sorry for them; I'd tied on one or two with that Wild Irish Rose and regretted living to regret it. At one time or another all of us at Monte Cassino had. The good nuns called it 'coming down with the flu,' and you have to admit the symptoms are very similar. My Santa Clara came down with the flu at least once a month. So did the other nuns. I concluded that in the convent Midol must have been harder to come by than wine.

Until we got to the island, I let the boys alone. The way they were groaning, I figured a lecture would be gilding the lily. It was only a little after four when we drove into the old corral, but Jonathan and Felicia stood sulking at the gate. "Late again with our supper," their reproachful eyes seem to say. The chickens, all eight of them I was glad to see, were busy finding supper for themselves in piles of road apples and cow patties, some fresh and steamy with heat in the cold. A table d'hote. I asked, "You guys wanna help me feed the animals?"

"Mnn mnn."

"No thanks."

"Why not? I thought you liked to help me with the animals."

Abel gagged and did a little dry heave off to the side of the road. Cain said, "I think we better go lie down, Sister."

"Why's that?"

He looked me in the eye, and he said, and you could tell it took some effort, "We have the flu coming on. Brk brk brk."

"Oh, the flu. I see. Okay. But I expect you to be well enough by seven to come down to the house and do your homework. I've got something for you."

So? I got a kick out of leaning on them a little. Why is it someone else's hangover always seems funny? But, like they say, what goes around comes around, and both Felicia and Jonathan began to lean on me soon as I came out of the barn with the grain bucket. I didn't move fast enough and Felicia, who has four perfectly good feet of her own, walked on one of mine for a step.

I was surprised to discover the hen's water hadn't frozen since I filled it in the morning. The light was getting bad and I couldn't see very well, but the water looked funny. An odd color. You might say, I thought, a Homeric color, as in 'the wine red sea.' I sniffed. What I suspected: Wild Irish Rose. One seventy-five a half gallon at Doug's Shop and Save and as good, apparently, for anti-freeze as it was for Mass. So, the children and the chicken had suffered from the same illness after all. Not botulism, however, but the Monte Cassino flu.

As I hobbled down the hill in the dim light of dusk, in the white on white glow of snow and ice, I noticed on top of the compost pile a dark mass, a new addition, something substantial. I went up close to see. Crowning the compost was Sister Agnes's entire generous donation of squash.

"What're we having for supper?" I asked coming into the warmth of the kitchen. "Squash?" I couldn't help myself. Sometimes I'm just bad. Santa Clara was cleaning her chain saw on the big oak dinner table.

"I'm fasting," she muttered. Meditating without her dinner was more like it.

"But today's only Monday," I observed. "You fast on Friday." She just kept on picking globs of pink sawdust out of her chain saw. Conversation-wise, Santa Clara seemed to have shot her bolt for the evening. So I made myself some boiled potatoes and yeast gravy with enough soy sauce to give it a salty tang and a lovely shade of gray. I had that and some chocolate milk.

Cain and Abel looked more themselves when they came down at seven. I gave them their flashcards with this word of advice, whispered softly in their little ears so that Santa Clara couldn't hear me. "If you little bastards don't memorize these friggin cards PDQ, you're gonna get the shit beat out of you. Trust me."

They didn't seem too worried, but they promised they would try. What Cain said, with a spark of the old Adam in his eye, was, "You got it, Chicken!"

When they had gone, and before I turned in for the night, I took another look at that 'poor man's' letter, the one whose mother had taught him about nuns, and who was praying to find peace with us starting tomorrow. It said: *i hev NOT HED wimin 4 sins i bin in jal hyr war u or nuns i no u no lots wimin 1 er 2 eler is fin i no yu wil do tis fer me i PRa fr u an peez god bles yu siters in kris.* Translation: 'Being nuns, you know lots of women. I haven't had a woman since they put me in the slammer. Get me one or two for tomorrow. I can hardly wait. God bless!'

"Clara," I said. "I think we may have a little problem about tomorrow."

"What is it now, Alex?" my Santa Clara inquired in that sweet, soft voice of hers I love so well.

CHAPTER FIFTEEN—SLATE BLUE

A sad color.

After the incident with the wine, we resolved to remove our supply for Mass from Trinity. Santa Clara volunteered to keep it. Talk about putting a fox to watch the chickens. We also got a CB. Adam and I spent Saturday fetching the radio from a farm in Lincoln. He had seen the ad for it in *Uncle Henry's*, a weekly magazine of Classifieds. On Thursday, when I picked the boys up at school I had managed to get an extension of my deadline from Mrs. Grater.

"Mrs. Grater," I said, wearing a big grin to signal my good news. "I found us a CB."

"Good," she said. "I'll call you in the morning. If I get through, the children can come to school."

"Well," I explained. "I'm not picking it up until Saturday."

"No problem," she said. "The children can enroll in school just as soon as I establish communication with Monte Cassino."

"Enroll? They are enrolled."

"Today they are. But not tomorrow. Friday was your deadline, Sister."

"But I've got us the CB." I showed her the ad. I had it circled in blue. Her lips, never large, pursed and disappeared. Her eyes narrowed scornfully. She knew, they told me, all

116

about circled ads in *Uncle Henry's*.

"And if it's already been sold?" she asked. "What then? I suppose then you would need a week's grace while you wait for the next issue of *Uncle Henry's*. I'm afraid not, Sister. I said Friday. I meant Friday. Friday is tomorrow, Sister. No CB tomorrow, no school tomorrow." This woman could get on my nerves.

"Mrs. Grater, it's a good price for a CB, and I've called him. He's holding it for us. But he lives up to Lincoln and he works days. Saturday's the soonest we could make arrangements to go for it. I mean, it's not like there's school on the weekend."

"I know when we have school, Sister."

I think Mrs. Grater missed her calling. She was made to be a Mother Superior. A Gauleiter, too, but opportunities like that don't come along every day.

"Er," I said, and then I had my inspiration. "I wanted you to know that wine we use for worship service? That the kids got into?" Her face set into lines even harder than before. I rushed on. "Well, Santa Clara's in charge of it now!"

"Santa Clara?" she asked, all ready to be sarcastic because of the 'Santa', which was a slip of the tongue due to me being nervous. But she was also a little charmed. You could tell, her lips reappeared. She almost smiled, being reminded like that of Santa Clara, our very own Mother Theresa.

I played up to the pleased little smile I saw hiding in the corners of her mouth. I mimicked a gesture I've seen Santa Clara use effectively many times. I lowered my face and modestly covered it with both my hands. I murmured, "Did I say Santa? That must be how I think of her." I peeked through my fingers. It had worked.

For a moment Mrs. Grater beamed. "Well," she said.

I dropped my hands and raised my head. I think I should have done this slower, like reluctantly. I made a mental note to practice. "It's okay?" I asked.

And she nodded, a little hesitant, realizing too late the price for having allowed herself, momentarily, to be charmed.

So we picked up the CB, Adam and I, on Saturday afternoon. We started out right after lunch, and headed up 1A there going toward Bangor. It was a wonder how Adam knew all these short-cuts: up 9, across the Penobscot at Old Town, and, when we got to the Lincoln area, he seemed just to kind of sense which fork to take, which dirt road to follow.

"You know these parts, Adam?" I asked. "I always thought you were from the mid-west."

"Naw," he said. "It's like a talent I have God gave me."

I should have known. "Maybe in another life. Maybe in another life you lived around here." He smirked.

We stopped at Doug's Shop & Save on the way home. I got a couple cans of chili to bring to supper and some nice brown bread sticks for Santa Clara to bring. Supper was excellent that evening. The Adams family prepared another terrific coq-au-vin. Like I said, Santa Clara brought bread sticks, still in the package and totally unharmed, as was Sister Agnes's donation of brown bread, still in the can. I managed to warm my chili without mishap and no one except Clara uncovered the half-breed spores she brought along. The pièce-de-résistance of the evening, however, was brought by Lennie and Virgie Soper, German Chocolate cake and Double Dutch chocolate ice-cream.

Virgie says she loves to cook for our community during the Black Fast because it's such a challenge. Besides the chocolate dessert, her contribution that night was One Bean Salad ("All I did was leave out the garbanzos and the green beans," she said), and an antipasto made with marinated eggplant rind ("I think," she said, "all the good stuff's in the rind.")

I was showing off the CB after supper. It was attached to the old car battery we used to run the TV.

It was Adam started the discussion about what handle we should use. "I guess," he said, "we could call ourselves the

Flying Nuns."

"None of that!" said Lennie and Sister Agnes together. Actually what I think Lennie said was "Nun of That!" and he meant it for a handle. Anyway, I laughed.

You could tell Santa Clara wasn't amused because she said, sourly, "Why don't we call ourselves The Adams Family?" Meaning, I guess, if it hadn't been for them we wouldn't have had to fork over fifty bucks for a CB when she wanted to buy herself a Belgian draft horse Beulah was trying to get rid of. Beulah had offered to teach her a course in Draft Horse Management for free. I was just as glad to postpone that for a while, not that I dislike Beulah.

"I think," said Cain, and I looked at his glass suspiciously because he doesn't usually talk up around grownups, except for me, and he regards me as a chicken. But his glass held milk. "I think Monte Cristo would be a good name."

Into the dead silence following his suggestion, I said, "Instead of Monte Cassino?" Then I had a great idea. "Hey," I said, "I got a great idea! Let's let Cain take charge of the CB and call ourselves Raising Cain." My suggestion fell as flat as Cain's had. But ideas started to flow: Spiritu Sanctu, St. Jude, St. X, Wild Irish Rose, Hot Toddy, Nun of This, Nun Such, Nun Sense, etc., etc.. I really did think my idea was best, especially since no one except Cain wanted to take responsibility for the radio, and every once in a while I repeated my suggestion. "Wouldn't it be poetic justice," I said, "for Cain to have the CB?"

Santa Clara finally snapped, "Would you please stop saying it would be poetic justice? You've had too much wine. If we got the CB so that Mrs. Grater could call us in an emergency, does it make any sense to give the CB to Cain?"

This, in case you didn't recognize it, was a rhetorical question. And everyone, except Cain and me, dutifully chorused "No, of course it doesn't make any sense!"

The crack about the wine, though, got me pissed and I went off to bed saying, "Suit yourself!"

Next morning the CB was gone. That's right, gone. Cain brought the news.

"What do you mean gone?" I said. It's true what they say about the bearers of bad news getting it. Poor Cain. He came down the hill about nine o'clock to tell us. Nine on Sunday morning. The one morning to lie around in bed, to make love, to eat toast and drink tea, to read the newspaper, like a whole vacation concentrated into a couple hours.

It hadn't always been so. When I first came to Monte Cassino, people dropped in to see my Santa Clara any time of the day or night, and every day of the week, even Sunday. Especially Sunday. Up in the barn, where we lived (except when Sister Benedict was on a Caribbean retreat), whenever someone came to see her, Santa Clara expected me to retire to my room, which, remember, was a chicken coop with a bed in it. Then Sister Agnes took to dropping in seven, seven-thirty Sunday mornings.

Finally one Saturday I bought a bolt for the door and told Santa Clara I'd seen signs of brown bear around the barn. We both knew bears will come in your house if they're hungry and smell food. So she didn't object to the bolt. And she didn't know that on my last trip to the out-house I tacked this sign to the door: NEVER ON SUNDAY. NO KNOCKING. NO ENTERING. THIS MEANS YOU. Next morning I heard Agnes scratching around at the door. I heard her try a couple times to open it.

Santa Clara said, "There's Sister Agnes. You better go to your room."

"Never on Sunday," I said. Then we got to doing something else pleasant and forgot all about Sister Agnes at the door. And that's how the Never On Sunday Rule was established. It was strictly enforced, I saw to that, even though on one or two occasions Santa Clara got to meditating at me pretty bad because of it.

So this Sunday morning, there was poor Cain breaking the Never On Sunday Rule, plus, on top of that, breaking the news that the CB was gone. Fifty dollars shot to hell. And how was I going to explain this to Mrs. Grater?

"Whadda ya mean it's gone?" I said. Santa Clara said I shouted. I do know I had Cain by the shoulders and was about to do to him what Toolshed Clara did to me the day I made pancakes out of her yeast spores.

Santa Clara stopped me. She said, "Who would like some hot chocolate? Let me make us some hot chocolate." She had climbed out of bed and put on a robe. Her hair was loose, falling in waves of red about her shoulders, making her look exposed, vulnerable, the way she did that first night in my apartment.

I dropped Cain. "Sorry," I said. I said, "Yeah. Hot chocolate sounds good." Cain and I looked at each other while Santa Clara busied herself at the stove. He and I would do that a lot—just look at each other—instead of talking. Cain, as you know, was ten, skinny, undernourished looking, and his complexion was bad. Since he began to live with us, he'd started wearing glasses, which didn't fit so good. They'd slip down his nose till they hit the end of it which, conveniently, turned up and stopped them falling off. Sometimes Cain would look at me in a particularly earnest way I had learned meant he knew something he wanted me to know, but which I had to figure out on my own. He had that look on his face that Sunday morning.

We sat at the big oak table with our hot chocolate and some bread we burn on the wood stove and call toast.

Santa Clara said in her soothingest voice, "Tell us what happened, Cain."

He stopped looking at me in that urgent way, kind of hauled his eyes off mine. He said, "Well, this morning, Abel and me we went to look at the CB. We wasn't gonna touch it or nothin'. Just look. Honest. But it weren't there. Father says it musta gone off with the generator." His eyes swung back to burden mine again. What was it he wanted me to know?

"Mrs. Grater's going to kill me," I said.

"She won't," said Cain.

"You know what I mean," I said.

"Yeah," said Cain. "She's gonna make you take us outta school." I didn't like to say in front of him I'd rather she would kill me. He didn't look too happy, either, about being taken out of school. And that, irrationally, annoyed me. "Dad says it went off with the generator and the skill saw," Cain elaborated, unhappily.

"And the roll roofing?" I asked. You see, in our little community, like in any big family, things would come up missing every now and then. When Scott was little, he always said a robber took the stuff he had mislaid. Then when whatever it was turned up, and his brothers and sister teased him, he would airily reply that the robber had brought it back. The robber at Monte Cassino, like Scott's robber, was thoughtful about returning all the little stuff, like the retractable measure, loppers and wire cutters, things like that. But not the generator. That disappeared the beginning of October. Or the skillsaw which walked a couple weeks later, not that it was much use without the generator. Roll roofing for the barn went one weekday in November while all of us were out applying for food stamps to see us through the winter.

Santa Clara continued the catalogue of missing items: the generator, the skill saw, the crowbar.

"No, not the crowbar," said Cain. His guilty knowledge was as plain as a flea on snow.

"Where's the crowbar, Cain?" I asked.

"I don't know, Sister," he mumbled.

"Cain!" Santa Clara cried, getting a look like Toolshed Clara about to avenge her spores. That crowbar is absolutely Santa Clara's favorite tool and every time it goes missing, she goes crazy.

"Take it easy," I suggested.

"I really don't know where it is, Sister," Cain lied.

"You better tell me what you know," threatened Clara.

I took Cain by the chin to make him look at me. "Cain?" I said with that little lilt grownups use to indicate to impressionable child that some heavy duty persuasion will ensue if they don't give in. "Cain, what do you know about Sister Clara's crowbar?"

Cain burst into tears, impressionable child's most effective defense against bullying adult.

"Leave him be, Alex," ordered Santa Clara, regaining her moral high ground.

Cain, snivelling, looked up at me, his eyes, beneath the tears, coolly assessing the situation.

Going for broke, I balled up my fist, displayed it prominently a few inches from Cain's oozing nose, and said, "The crowbar!"

"In the pasture," he said.

"In the pasture?" said Santa Clara and I.

"It was an accident," said Cain.

"It was an accident?" we said.

Cain burst into tears again, but we didn't.

Santa Clara said, coldly, "Show me."

I said, "Why don't we get dressed first."

Twenty minutes later we met up at the barn. Cain led us around to the back pasture. "There," he said, pointing at nothing. "It's over there."

One day right before Thanksgiving, he and Abel had borrowed it he said. "We needed to make a cave to play Ali Baba."

"You mean," said Santa Clara, "to play forty thieves." She really was attached to that crowbar.

"Yeah?" I said. "And then what happened?"

"You rang the bell and, uh, it got left. Then it snowed."

"But why didn't you tell someone?" asked Santa Clara. "Why didn't you come tell me?"

He looked at her like she had a booger hanging off her nose. "I guess we forgot," he muttered.

"You guess you forgot!" Santa Clara sighed as Job must

once have sighed. "Well," she said, resignedly, "at least we know where it is."

On our way past the barn, we stopped to feed the animals. In the lean-to, I discovered another pitiful pile of feathers and down, and, sure enough, only seven chickens came to scramble in the snow for the grain I flung to them.

"Maybe you should consider getting another rooster," Santa Clara suggested.

"Maybe," I conceded. "But roosters are bullies. Besides," I laughed, "it would seem unfaithful."

"Unfaithful?" echoed Santa Clara, as if the word was new to her vocabulary.

That Sunday was the Super Bowl, and everyone had been planning to come watch it with us down at Immaculate Conception. But after worship service Saturday night, Santa Clara said, "For half-time I'll make us Dynamites." Which roused everyone's interest. Then she continued, "It's a recipe of my mother's." Remembering Santa Clara's mother's biscuits, people started having second thoughts about coming to our Super Bowl party. That's when Santa Clara blew it. She said, I guess to reassure them, "It's good food."

I couldn't help feeling sorry for her. "Hey!" I said, "they're only Sloppy Joes." People still looked doubtful, so I said I would buy it canned. "What can go wrong ?" I asked. No one answered. But they did agree to come. That Sunday morning, after we had fed the animals, as soon as we got back down to the house, Clara started taking out pots and pans like she was going to cook for an army. "What's up?" I asked.

"Well," said Santa Clara, "I have to make my Dynamites."

I said, "But I'm supposed to buy them."

"Oh, no," said Santa Clara. "I'm going to make them. There's all that good hamburger I want to use up."

"What good hamburger?" I asked.

"Never mind," said Santa Clara.

"Not that hamburger I bought two weeks ago... "

"It's good food," said Santa Clara. Her mole showed signs

of acting up so I climbed the hill, not sure what I should do. First thing that happened was Toolshed Clara collared me. Not literally; I'd learned to be more careful.

"We're leaving," she said majestically.

Was this a royal we, or was Jaspers going too, I wondered. "Oh, really?" I said.

"No!" said Clara "It's no good trying to persuade us to stay. Our mind is made up."

Seeing it was a safe thing to say, I said again, "Oh, really?"

"I assure you, Sister, it's no use to beg. We are going to a community where the artist is understood. And her problems are appreciated!"

"Well," I said.

"We will," she told me, "be ready to leave immediately after breakfast in the morning."

I went back to "Oh, really?" again.

"It's outside of Starks," she said. "They told me it shouldn't take you more than three hours to get us there. That's allowing time for maintenance. I described your truck to them." Every silver lining has its cloud, I observed.

The Super Bowl that night was exciting, I guess. Everyone fell asleep way before it was over. The score was close, fourteen to thirteen, we found out next day. I'm not sure just why we all conked out. It might have been the air. Does methane make you drowsy? Ten minutes after we ate those Dynamites that Santa Clara made with the two-week-old hamburger, everyone started cutting farts. Alexander's Ragtime Band. Good thing none of us smoked. We'd've gone up in a fireball if someone'd lighted a match. I remember thinking, as I drifted off to sleep, that must be how they got the name, Dynamite.

Cain was kind of clinging all through the game, which wasn't like him. And he fell asleep with his head in my lap. After the game was over, Adam made fun of him. Cain didn't say a word, he just kept looking at me, the way he did when he told me the CB was gone.

125

I woke up late Monday morning and quickly realized I would have to hustle if I wanted to get the animals fed before I took the kids over to the bus stop. I was surprised, as I topped the hill, not to find Cain waiting impatiently for me. It took a moment to register that the truck was gone. Then I saw that the door to Trinity stood open, a chicken industriously scratching in the snow drifted across the threshold. Inside it was bitterly cold. It looked like the Adams family had left in a hurry, and it was clear they didn't plan to return: the only piece of furniture left seemed to be the iron stove. Toolshed Clara was very put out about the truck being gone. "So inconsiderate," she said, "that sort are. What are you going to do, Sister?" she asked, "about getting us to Starks this morning?"

Along about three that afternoon Sheriff Lennie Soper drove over to the island. The little Datsun with its medals of St. Christopher and St. Jude had turned up in the Food Star parking lot in Bangor. I had to go identify it. Toolshed Clara said to hurry. "We still can make it to Sparks, Sister," she said, "if you hurry. So, hurry!"

We didn't make it to Sparks until the next afternoon. Toolshed Clara's new community consisted of three families who were homesteading on about two hundred acres of land. They had some road frontage, so there was a telephone, and one of the houses even had electricity. They took us around to show us the buildings, the barn, a community sauna they had made. In the last house, in the corner, stood a generator. Not just any old generator. The generator that had disappeared from Monte Cassino the previous October. How could I tell it was ours? There's this little dent in the casing where Felicia hauled off to kick me one morning and missed.

"Where'd you get this generator?" I asked.

"Uncle Henry's," my host replied.

"Up around Lincoln?" I asked.

"Yep. A farm up there. He was upgrading his. We got a

good price on it."

"I bet you did," I said.

"Kind of hard to find the place," he reminisced.

"Yeah," I said. "Isn't it?"

Well, as soon as I got back home, I went over to see Sheriff Lennie Soper and told him all about it. We eventually got our CB back. Our CD? Well, no one else claimed it, and Santa Clara wanted, in the worst way, to sell it so she could buy Beulah's draft horse.

"Maybe," I suggested, "if we advertise in *Uncle Henry's* for them, the Adams family will come back and we can go into business together. Think," I said, "of all the draft horses you could buy then." No one thought that was funny.

"Well," said Sister Agnes, who had dropped in, "I think it should be a rule we don't take murderers, rapists, arsonists, or people who steal from us."

"What about loiterers?" I asked. Santa Clara's sigh told me I was getting to be a pain in the ass again.

Trinity stayed empty the rest of that winter; we held community suppers down at Immaculate Conception. It wasn't until April that we cleaned it up for a new family. It smelled something awful when I opened up the door and went in. Mrs. Grater-like, I followed my nose to two plastic garbage bags in the bedroom. One held down, the other feathers, about six chickens worth of each. But, I kept reminding myself, those coqs-au-vin were awfully good.

I think a lot about Cain and Abel. Especially Cain. Especially early in the morning when all the world's asleep. Except me. Except maybe, somewhere, him.

CHAPTER SIXTEEN—BLACK

Okay. Time again for black!

Black as in mourning? Or like 'black and secret hags'? Actually, now that I'm to this point in my story, I could maybe not use black at all. I could use... Ochre. Like earth color. Because, setting it all down like I have, Santa Clara's slow drifting away—I was out on Monte Cassino some three years—her growing coolness, her more frequent meditations at me, they all seem more like just part of that inevitable cycle of life. But at the time! Well, you'll see. I think, after all, I'll stick to black.

Storm report: Nothing's changed.

Remember the blizzard of, when was it, '78? That three-day blizzard when they shut down Boston for two weeks. Up here in Maine it wasn't so bad, only snowed for a day. A day and a night. Sister Benedict's batteries are dead, (surprise, surprise) so I don't know what's happening in the rest of the world, but it's been snowing here at Monte Cassino for twenty-four hours now. I had trouble a minute ago getting out of the house, so much snow had piled up against the door. I brought in lots of wood, enough to last two more days. After that, the furniture! It's a little after five and dark, of course.

Mr. Chester Brown, if that is his name, is resting comfortably. It's weird how you get used to things. Yesterday at this time I was really freaked being here alone with his body. Now I'm beginning to feel sleepy. I'll write this last story, then I think I'll try to get some shut-eye. It's going on thirty-six hours since I've slept.

Next: How Alex Adler, that nice (partly) Jewish girl from the Bronx, came down with the Sister Benedict Syndrome. I'm getting punchy, need some sleep.

The rest of the winter was uneventful. Sister Benedict came home the first of March, the beginning of spring. Well, some people were tapping maple trees, that farm on Route 15, for instance, there by Newalls Orchard. Where Chester Brown used to stake out the place. But more about that later.

Sister Benedict, as usual, looked beautiful: tanned and rested. And clean compared to the rest of us. Her skin was smooth and fresh looking. No Black Fast for her those two months each year on the Caribbean. Which seems to me unfair when you think she has black beans to work with and they taste good. But, as Santa Clara always says, Sister Benedict is a good woman. And so are her parents. Who, remember, own that part of Central America that Standard Fruit doesn't. Her parents are good for about fifteen thousand a year to Monte Cassino, too.

Despite how good she was and all, Sister Benedict did not get on with Sister Agnes. In fact, ever since Sister Agnes first arrived at Monte Cassino, and she and Santa Clara took to spending all their time together, Sister Benedict had treated Sister Agnes shitty. The same way she had treated Beulah the year before. The same way, come to think of it, Agnes had been treating me ever since I arrived and took up residence in the chicken coop.

Toward the end of April, I got a letter from Scott saying he was coming to Maine and could he spend a week at Monte Cassino because he had something important to discuss with Sister Clara. He was bringing a friend he said. Since

Scott's been known to show up with a van-load of friends with no notice whatsoever, I suspected this friend was more than a friend and I was curious. He said to expect him May 15, which is the day I think of as our anniversary, Santa Clara's and mine. It was on the 15th of May she came to visit me the first time and I said to her —she was sitting on the kitchen chair, looking so sweet in her flannel nightie, running her lovely hands through her hair to dry it—that is I heard myself saying, "I got your room fixed up, but maybe you'd just as soon sleep with me."

I was eager to see Scott. In the days and weeks after the Adams Family took a powder, I discovered I was lonely on the island without Cain and Abel. Especially at night I found I missed them. Santa Clara seemed to have fallen on meditative ways, and without the boys to badger in the evenings, most nights I had no one to talk with.

A typical evening might go something like this:

"It says in this article that according to the Bureau of Labor Statistics, working in the woods is the country's most dangerous occupation." That's me talking.

Santa Clara: "…"

Me: "Probably one reason that doesn't bother you a lot is you think it's all in God's hands anyway."

Santa Clara: "…"

Me: "It says anyone who works in the woods should wear a hard hat at least. If I got you a hard hat, Clara, would you wear it? I sure wish you would. That bandanna's cute, but…"

Santa Clara: "…"

Me: "It says you should never work in the woods alone. D'you ever think of working with Beulah? I bet she would. Maybe you could work with her at her place a week, and then she could come here and work a week. I worry about you all alone cutting down trees. What if something happened? You know it's possible."

Santa Clara: "…"

Me: "Do you know what's playing in Ellsworth? *Gone With*

the Wind. D'you ever see that? I know it's politically incorrect, but isn't that some movie?

"Do you like Leslie Howard? Did you ever see, what's the name of that movie? Anyway, it's Leslie Howard and Dame Wendy Hillyer. This was before she was Dame Wendy Hillyer, of course. Actually they were in two terrific movies together. *Pygmalion.* But the other one I can't remember the name of it. But I like it at least as well. They sing this song: *I know where I'm going. And I know who's going with me. I know who I love, But the Lord knows who I'll marry.*

"I love you, Santa Clara. And I'd love to go to the movies with you. You wanna go see *Gone With the Wind*? Maybe Agnes and Benedict would like to go. What do you think?"

Santa Clara: "..."

"I'm going to bed."

Weekday nights we always watched re-runs of M.A.S.H. after supper, so that was more like someone else was in the house, I mean she'd laugh at Radar and stuff. At first I used to ask her what was wrong, but all she ever said was "Nothing." Or, "For crying out loud, Alex, nothing." Or, "Alex, I'm meditating."

So, it wasn't any big surprise when in April, about the time I got the letter from Scott, Santa Clara said one evening that she thought it would be a good idea if I took up residence in the tool shed. I'll say this for the tool shed: it didn't smell of chicken shit. And you could argue, as I did, that I could just as easily talk to myself there as I could in the barn. But I felt awful. Each morning after I did the chores, I spent an hour or so fixing up the chicken coop. I got it really clean and floored it, put in insulation. I walled it with clean cedar shakes so it looked good and smelled, for a change, wonderful.

I was going to propose, once it was ready, that I stay there, in my old room, like the only reason I moved was to make these renovations. I planned to make this proposal to Santa Clara on our Anniversary. You see, once I moved out of the barn, it was like Sister Agnes moved in. She was always there with Santa Clara. They had dinner together, and they watched M.A.S.H. together, and Sister Agnes took to bringing two dishes to community supper, one for her and one for Santa Clara. Both made with freshly opened canned goods and edible. The silver lining, I guess, my mother is always going on about.

Well, May 15 came and went with no Scott. Altogether, the day did not go as I had imagined it. I bought Santa Clara two dwarf apple trees for an Anniversary present. She wanted to start an orchard. Two trees weren't much, but they were a beginning. I thought they would be a symbol of a new beginning for us.

As it turned out, I never even saw Santa Clara on May 15. At six in the morning I tried to bring her a cup of tea in bed, like old times, but she'd shot that frigging bear bolt I'd installed against Sister Agnes.

I planted that day. Miserable job in May. That's when the black flies start. And it was cold and wet. My hair soon was plastered not only with fly dope, but with dead flies and mud. I was paying no attention to what I was doing, just sticking in seeds at random, my body a quivering antenna trying to locate Santa Clara.

Early on I heard her saw buzzing up on Soper's Ridge. Then from about ten to ten-thirty I heard nothing at all. I imagined her concussed from a tree falling on her. I saw her lying in a pool of blood, limbed by her own chainsaw.

Just when I thought I could stand it no longer, I saw Virgie Soper arrive in the family car. I decided to play it cool. Maybe I could catch Clara for lunch. But next thing, Clara sailed right on past the barn with Virgie, and headed out toward the spit. I'd played it wrong. God knows where she was off to. Like Onan, I scattered my seed on the ground, and I ran to the barn. Sister Benedict was standing at the corral in a swarm of black flies. Brain doodling.

"What's up?" I panted. She looked at me lazily, one eyebrow raised. Patience-of-a-Saint. She said nothing. Some day a nun simpering at me like that is going to find herself flat on her back. "Where'd they go?" I asked.

She shrugged.

"Benedict! Answer me!" I suggested. Wildly.

"What do you want to know?" she said, all soft and sweet.

"What do I want to know? Are you deaf? Where did they go?"

"With Virgie, I guess."

I thought for a moment. "Who went with Virgie?"

"Clara and Agnes."

"Do you know when they'll be back?"

"They didn't say. Tomorrow, maybe."

"Tomorrow!"

"Or Sunday."

"Sunday!"

"They got a ride with Virgie to Boston.They're going to visit Clara's brother," she volunteered.

Clara's brother lives in Boston. She hates her brother. I took the dwarf apple trees and I tucked them into Santa Clara's bed, the one that's built into the wall like a bathtub. I put one facing the wall, and the other facing into the room. I put a note on the pillow: *Happy Anniversary, year three of forever.*

While I was writing notes, I decided to write one to Scott, in case he came while I was gone, because I'd decided to get the hell out of there for a while. My note to Scott said, *Hi, Scott. Welcome. You and your friend can stay in the two retreat houses. I've gone to Kelley's. Be back soon. Mother.* I nailed it to the tool shed door because that's where Scott usually stays when he comes to visit. It was kind of a vain hope he would ever read it, though. He would see it. He would even hold it in his hands. But read it? Unh, unh. For some reason, none of the children ever read my notes. It's been one of life's great disappointments.

I can remember how eagerly I used to wait for the time

when I would not always have to be with them, but could write to them instead: *Wash your hands. Your snack is in the fridge. I'll be home at 4:00.* Or: *Please take the clothes out of the dryer as soon as you get home.* Or: *You're to call Jeremy's mother. Something about a broken window.*

The snack would always have disappeared, but one look at the refrigerator door and you knew they didn't read the part about washing their hands. Forget about the clothes in the dryer. Jeremy's mother and I always managed to work things out between us: broken windows, missing change, dirty words.

But I left the note for Scott anyway and then I walked to Kelley's. Kelley's is a little restaurant on Route 15 about two miles from Monte Cassino. I pigged out on pecan pie and vanilla ice cream. Which didn't do me any good. But the walk did. I still felt miserable when I got home. Scott and his friend hadn't come and I was disappointed. They didn't show up at all that day.

Saturday I was to pick up some resawn lumber in Eddington. A project of Santa Clara's. Plus a couple squares of cedar shingles for me, to finish off the chicken coop. I still hoped to move back in. In the saner light of morning, I realized I would stand a better chance if I made different arrangements for presenting my Anniversary present to Santa Clara. So I sacrificed my set of clean sheets to a harmonious future and removed the trees to the doorstep. I even swept her floor. I also changed the note. After much consideration, I decided on: *Happy May 15. I hope your orchard is fruitful and lasts forever.* 'Lasts forever.' Get it?—How long Santa Clara said, that first morning-after, she wanted to be with me.

And I left another note for Scott on the tool shed door saying when I expected to be home—by two—and telling him and his friend they were to stay in the two retreat houses.

Sister Benedict was nowhere to be seen all day. Usually on Saturday morning we all get together about nine-thirty to plan our workday together. But what with Clara and Agnes both gone, I guess Benedict had decided to take the day off. Which was all right with me.

The trip to Eddington and back takes about four hours, and I'd as soon shingle as muck out the barn for what was left of the day. I left Monte Cassino about ten taking the little Datsun truck with my friends St. Christopher and St. Jude. It was back roads all the way so, except for stalling out right there in the lumber-yard, I didn't have any problems. It was a beautiful day, new leaves all lacy in the trees, those little propellers from the maples spinning golden in the air, birds everywhere, sweet creamy clouds drifting across a Delft blue sky.

I forgot my troubles, forgot about Santa Clara and Sister Agnes and living by myself in the tool shed. I started whistling that tune from Don Giovanni, the one where he's seducing Zerlina, and I sang the words while I unloaded the lumber and put the shingles in the chicken coop, gave the animals a snack, all that kind of stuff. Didn't see a soul. In my imagination Santa Clara's fruit orchard had grown to maturity, and so had we, blissfully, together.

Whistling, I swung down the path to the tool shed and threw open the door. There, lying in my bed in a steamy embrace was my son Scott and what appeared to be a woman twice his age. The reason I say this is she was gray, at least as gray as I am. One of her eyes, it would have been her right eye, was looking straight into mine. Her head was nestled in the hollow of Scott's shoulder, that would be his left shoulder, which was bare, like the rest of him. She said, quite clearly when you consider her mouth was smack up against Scott's chest, "Don't you ever knock?"

I'm not sure what I said. Probably "I'm sorry." I backed out and shut the door. My note, I noticed belatedly, was gone. So I guess I should've known: Scott had come and it was never in the cards he was going to read what I had written to him.

I hate walking in on people making love. I discovered. I went and started shingling the chicken coop. I cut my finger trying to break the wire that binds the square. I hit my thumb with the hammer. I couldn't find the level so my first row was off a little. By the time Scott and his friend found me, the lines of shingles sagged noticeably earthward, marked here and there by rust colored dots of drying blood.

"Those shingles aren't straight, you know," she said.

"Hi, Mom," said Scott. They were standing in the doorway together, holding each other around the waist. Blocking my light. "Mom, I want you to meet Anne. She's the friend I wrote you about."

With motherly continuity, I replied, "Didn't you read my note?"

"Yeah, I read it."

"What did it say?"

"Oh, Mom!" This is a generic exchange, by the way. We developed it decades ago. "Anne works with me," Scott said when we were done. "She's a paralegal too." Then he said, "Why don't you come on out of there?"

So I did, and we sat in the sun and the flies for a while. Anne is not twice Scott's age. She's just prematurely gray. She's no more than half again as old as he is, probably. Late '30s. And quite beautiful.

They were sorry to hear about me and Santa Clara, and Scott was sorry he hadn't read my note 'more carefully.' They were just excited, you know, being here, and he'd just assumed I would put them in the tool shed, and no one was around, you know. Anne didn't say much, just sort of looked a lot. You could tell Scott was in love, head-over-heels, but that Anne, she was some cool lady. She made me feel like Holden Caulfield on a big date. My hands, my feet, my tongue, they all seemed several sizes too big. And the clumsier I was, the more amused she seemed to be. Not 'ha ha, look at this klutz you call your mother' amused. More of a world-weary smile in the corner of the eye because nothing at all can astonish me any longer kind of amused. A 'those shingles aren't straight you know,' sort of superiority. A willingness to overlook-being-interrupted-making-love species of condescension.

Scott and Anne stayed a week. What they'd come for was to activate the Central American Underground Railroad. Sister Agnes and Santa Clara didn't get back until Sunday afternoon. I had kept Santa Clara's orchard watered and on Sunday morning I renewed the note in the branches. I didn't change the wording: *Happy May 15. I hope your orchard is fruitful and lasts forever.* But I added a red heart with a stub of crayon I found in my pocket, the pocket with the patch reading KEEP CALM KEEP CALM KEEP CALM.

Around three o'clock I moseyed over to the barn to ask Santa Clara to come to dinner. "Scott's cooking," I said. I said, "He brought a friend. Anne. She works with him down in Harlingen. With refugees. That's what they want to talk with you about. About the refugees. Whether we could help them get into Canada." Santa Clara was sitting on her doorstep where earlier in the day her orchard had been. She was working on Jonathan's bridle, mending it with some twine. "Will you come?" I asked.

She squinted up at me. "Come?" she said.

"To dinner. I just told you. Scott's here. He and this friend he brought, Anne, they want to talk with you about refugees. Helping them into Canada. Will you come?"

She looked very pensive. Finally she said, "What time?"

"Whenever. Five? Six? What's good for you?"

I think she said, "I can't stay." She had her face stuck in the bridle and twine so it was hard to hear her.

"Well," I looked at my watch, "it's three now. Is five too late?"

"Five's okay," she conceded.

I started back toward the tool shed. She hadn't said boo about the apple trees. But I sure wasn't going to give her the satisfaction of mentioning them first. No way.

It was kind of like that first night in my Hallowell apartment when all of a sudden I heard a voice that sounded like mine saying, "I got your room fixed up, but maybe you'd just as soon sleep with me." There on the cool afternoon air I heard my voice saying, "You get the apple trees?"

Of course then I had to look around to see what she would say. She didn't lift her head or anything. What she said is, "What apple trees?"

"The two apple trees I left on your steps."

"Oh, those apple trees."

"They're to start your orchard."

"I wondered who left them."

It's true. I hadn't signed my name.

The dinner went smoothly. Scott made a stir-fry with tofu. I baked a squash pie. Anne threw together a salad. She and Santa Clara got along like a house on fire, which seemed to please Scott immensely. In fact, around nine o'clock when he went off to bed, the two of them retired to the barn to 'finish making plans.' The plans they made involved a sixteen year-old Guatemalan boy, Eduardo, a Mayan Indian. Scott, they decided, should return to Texas for Eduardo, who was in Sanctuary, while Anne stayed on at Monte Cassino.

When Scott returned with Eduardo, he and Anne would drive the boy across into Canada. It wasn't secret or dangerous or anything. Not like bringing refugees across the Mexican border into the country, Scott explained. In fact, going into Canada, you let immigration know and they set up a court hearing, so it was all legal and above board. To keep it legal, Scott and Anne, being paralegals, wanted to be there. Scott was to be gone a week.

Anne and Santa Clara spent a couple days in New Brunswick setting up a place for Eduardo to stay. As it worked out, Scott came down with the flu, at least that's what Anne told me, and Eduardo ended up coming on his own. Anne and Santa Clara picked him up in Bangor at the Greyhound Bus Station one morning around three o'clock and brought him back to Monte Cassino. He had made his way all on his own to San Diego from the village in Guatemala where he was born. The military had wiped out his village he said. He had seen his mother and two of his brothers murdered. He had no idea whether anyone else in his family was still alive. He had hoped, if they were, to find them or hear word of them in the Guatemalan community in San Diego. A church group took him in and started him on the road to Canada, by way of Texas and now Maine.

On a Friday morning early in June, Eduardo, Santa Clara and Anne started off for Canada. A week later I got a card from Fredericton. Well, not me exactly. The card was addressed to Monte Cassino, and it said, *Delayed. Back soon. Eduardo fine. Clara.*

A couple days later, around four in the afternoon, I drove up to the barn in that little Datsun pick-up truck with all the saints on the dashboard. What did I see but Santa Clara's truck in the barnyard. They were back! I climbed out my window and charged up the path. I flung open the door to Santa Clara's room and deja vu! there was that eye of Anne's peering at me, this time nestled in the hollow of Santa Clara's shoulder. Her hair glinted silver beside the brick red of Santa Clara's hair, which was loose and cascading wildly down her back. They were standing there in the middle of the room, the way two people do, space enough between them to slide a piece of paper, onion skin. I just stood there with my face hanging out, not moving or anything. Neither did they. Then, don't ask me why, I reached up and rapped on the inside of the door. I said, "Knock, knock." Like any ass-hole might in a similar situation.

Anne's voice when she spoke was really quite distinct when you stop to think her mouth was slap up against Santa Clara's neck. She said, "When I said knock before you come in, I meant knock on the outside of the door." Like I said in a previous chapter, what goes around comes around. I tried to stick it out, as Benedict, Beulah, and Agnes had done before me. But the day after Anne and Santa Clara returned from Canada, Anne moved into the chicken coop. After that, whenever Santa Clara spoke to me, she called me Anne. The Sopers came to dinner that next Saturday, and after dinner I went home with them. Until I got stuck with that stupid body two days ago, I haven't spent a single night out here at Monte Cassino since then.

CHAPTER SEVENTEEN—LEMON YELLOW

For a nasty fellow.

I met Chester Brown the following Tuesday. The reason I'm not sure that's his real name is whenever he signs a note, he signs it with his initials and the initials are not C.B.. They're C.P., and not P on its way to becoming B, but P with the last stroke sailing off toward the bottom left corner of the page. How I know this is, starting that Tuesday he was my boss. Well, Tommy Gross, one of Sheriff Lennie Soper's foster kids (former foster kid, Tommy's nearly thirty) was my boss, but we were doing a job for this Chester Brown, building a deck and patio behind his house. The first week off-island I spent at Soper's sharing a bedroom with newly arrived twins, traumatized twins, age seven. After two nights I was a basket case, they kept having these weird nightmares. So on Saturday I moved. With Soper's help. A lot of it. They supplied the up-front cash, a beat-up old mattress, bedding and kitchen utensils. My stuff, having achieved a collective identity, remained at Monte Cassino.

My apartment was another one-roomer, no Murphy bed, but a sunny view of the harbor with lobster boats and sail boats, and it smelled of lilac from a huge bush outside. Not having sulky animals to push me around soon as I woke up in the morning was disorienting at first, but I began to take long, solitary walks down to the dock, and after a few days some of the fisher folk began to acknowledge me and I'd pass the time with them until they sailed or I had to get back to go to work.

How I got this job with Tommy is his partner was in jail. For drunk and disorderly, and apt to be there for a while. Whenever Rollie got drunk, which was weekends, he most always raised a little hell. More often than not, someone landed in hospital. Someone, but never Rollie. That's why, when it crossed my mind it might not be a squirrel up in the loft but Rollie, I didn't investigate. Say it had been Rollie. I figured, he was willing not to bother about me, I sure as hell wasn't going to make an issue of his being there.

This last time Rollie sent a fellow to the emergency room, the judge said enough already and sentenced him to a year. Except for a few of his victims, everyone thought this was unfair, so none of the guys would take his job. The Sopers thought where I was a woman and from away and had gray hair, I could get away with it. Besides, Tommy needed the help. Tommy and I had worked some together out to Monte Cassino and we got along okay. It was a good solution for us both. Tommy said he'd pick me up mornings, no problem, it was on his way. Mr. Brown's house is on Alternate One, on the way to Bangor, on Green Lake. That Tuesday, my first day at work, was drizzly, like it had been all spring. The windshield kept getting steamed up with our breath.

"Wish it would clear," I said.

"Eyup."

"Black flies bad out there where we're goin'?"

"Eyup."

"They don't bother you?"

He wobbled his hand. "So so."

"Who is this guy? What's his name?"

"Brown. Chester Brown. Works in Bangor I guess."

"Family?"

"I never seen no one. Never seen him except the day he

hired me. Leaves notes. Funny."

While Tommy stepped into the bushes to get rid of his morning coffee, I read Chester Brown's note for that Tuesday. It said, 'I thought I told you not to sink the nails. I'm not paying for this.'

"What's he say?" said Tommy, emerging from the woods, settling his trousers round his hips in a satisfied way. "Bitching 'cause I did his floor right?"

"Eyup. I thought you said his name's Chester Brown."

"I did. It is."

"Then how comes he signed this C.P.?"

"C. P.? I dunno. Never noticed."

After that I used to call Chester Brown our Communist Party boss, which, when you know the whole story, you'll find ironic.

That first week living alone again was hard. I'd stroll down the hill from my apartment to the dock in the early morning, watch the sun come up, mark the southern-most bit of shore on Long Island where it rose on the solstice, dreading to see, through the long days of summer, the sun's slow retreat south, feeling sorry for myself in June for how lonely I would be in December. Then Saturday came and nothing to do because Mr. Brown didn't want us around on the weekend. Lennie asked didn't I want to go with him and Virgie out to Monte Cassino. I said no, I was busy. I climbed Blue hill and let the black flies eat me.

Around eight that evening, the landlord knocked on my door. He said I had a phone call. It was Lennie. Lennie said did I know anyone willing to feed the animals out to Monte Cassino for a few days.

"What's up?" I asked.

"No one's gonna be there."

"Oh yeah?" I said, suggestively.

"Yeah."

Since indirection had gotten me nowhere, I asked, "Where're people going to be?"

He told me Sister Agnes was going to be visiting her family in up-state New York, and Sister Benedict was planning to spend a week at her Mother House in Rhode Island (not to be confused with her mother's house in the Caribbean). Sister Anne and Sister Clara would be gone too.

"Anne's not a Sister. Neither is Clara," I pointed out, crossly.

"They're still not going to be there," Lennie said. And he still wasn't telling me what I wanted to know: where the two of them were going and whether they were going there together. "Beulah said she'd take care of 'em Sunday, tomorrow. And Sister Benedict'll be back Wednesday most probably."

"Benedict and Jonathan don't get along," I said.

"Maybe so. But Sister Benedict says she'll feed 'em, evenings at least, soon as she gets home. Which most likely will be Wednesday. Says mornings she needs to herself, for prayin'. So, it's mornings people are worried about. And Monday and Tuesday night."

I said, "Why doesn't Clara stay home if she's worried?" I didn't know how much Lennie and Virgie knew or suspected about why I had left Monte Cassino. It was clear they didn't want to hear about it. It was for sure unfair to unload my resentments onto Lennie.

Lennie said, "Well, Alex, I think it's important. And I'll tell you about it when I see you. If you think of anyone, give me a ring."

"Don't hang up," I said. "I'll do it."

"Goo-wud, then. I'll let 'em know."

"Yeah." It turned out where they were going was to Arizona for a load of refugees. So I was glad I said yes. Lennie explained, when he saw me, he was afraid to say anything on the phone 'cause he had a slight suspicion it might be tapped. Coming from the sheriff, I took it as probable.

He and Virgie came by Sunday afternoon to deliver my favorite truck, the little brown Datsun with all the saints and stuff.

"They was hopin' you'd say yes," Lennie explained. "They said seein's how you don't have wheels, you might like to have the use of the truck."

So, Monday at four-thirty I was down to the spit. Luckily, all that week the tide was so I could just drive across. The island looked beautiful in the early morning light, Soper's Ridge draped in dove gray mist, the sky behind the softest pink. The pointed firs, standing stolid along the shore, seemed to me like arms embracing the little community beyond Tromp l'oeil. The sharp black firs looked forbidding as fixed bayonets, and the pink sky tawdry as rouge on a clown.

The truck stalled out on me or I probably would have turned around and gone back home. But, I decided, with my buddies St. Christopher and St. Jude to look after me, I'd be okay. They'd seen me through some situations worse than this. Jonathan and Felicia were waiting for me at the old corral. They seemed glad to see me. I found myself missing Stupor Mundi unreasonably. And I refused to think about Cain.

When I had finished with my chores, I went into Santa Clara's room. To make myself some coffee, to leave a note, to rub in some salt. Beulah, it seemed, had already left a note for Clara. I don't know how it is with other people, but I am a compulsive reader. I can't go to the can without a book in hand, and, caught short, I read labels on jars in the medicine cabinet. Plus, in this instance, I was curious. I struggled, briefly, with my conscience and then I read Beulah's note. It said: *Whoever stacked your hay made a mess of it. You got mold. That's how come J wheezes. Was afraid to toss it fencing the way it is they'd just break through and eat it all. Whoever got your chicken feed paid too much and poor quality to boot. You want Blue Seal.*

Well, yours truly stacked the hay, and yours truly bought the chicken feed. I mulled it over while I drank my coffee. It was still only five-thirty. Tommy wasn't due to pick me up for an hour and a half. I made up my mind. And I left this note: *Sorry about the mold. That's the hay we got from Drinkwater. I took all the bad bales and put them out in the boulders beyond the spring where you're thinking of building a field barn next year. Jonathan never goes over there... & I fixed the fence.* Going to Agway for the chicken feed was Santa Clara's idea, but I doubted she'd remember that. So after some hesitation I wrote: *Getting chicken meal at Agway was your idea.* Then I tore that part off and stuffed it in my pocket.

Altogether, about fifteen bales were moldy. I tossed them out onto the truck, which is a whole lot easier than tossing them from the truck up into the barn. Don't I hate haying! Still, I felt a pang of grief that I wouldn't be doing it that summer. Jonathan, being naturally curious, started across the pasture to see where I was going with all that hay, but he lost interest at the creek, still swollen with spring run-off.

I dropped the fifteen bales down some crevices between boulders, then covered the holes with armfuls of leaf mold and spruce branches. Just in case Jonathan should amble over later to investigate. The fence was down where I suspected it would be. It's electric and in one place especially the distance between supports is just too long. A stiff breeze nearly always blows it down. I turned off the charger and spliced it one more time.

On my way out I stopped and rewrote my note. The first part I kept the same, but I'd thought of a more tactful way to address Beulah's charge about the chicken feed. I just said: *Using Agway meal wasn't my idea.*

I drove out on the highway a little before seven. The day was still unspoiled, still drifting out of sleep. I surprised a fox in the field by Newalls. He seemed to dissolve in the play of light, green and gold, in the field of growing grass and dandelions. A van, jaringly new in that run-down stretch of highway, stood on the verge of the road. The driver, wearing a suit and tie, his hat tipped over his brow, seemed to be catching forty winks. It seemed odd.

Talk about leaving notes; Chester Brown, the guy on the sofa downstairs, the one we were building the deck for, left the damndest notes for Tommy and me. Every day he left one, all signed C.P.. Tommy said he never read them any more, they were all ca ca. (That's what he said: ca ca. Soper kids don't talk dirty.) But I read them. The compulsive reader in me. The man did nothing but bitch. He bitched we went too slow. He bitched we did things right. He bitched we did things wrong (like poop in the woods—once). But he wouldn't let us in the house. I don't think it was our poop anyway, because in the first place it only happened the once, and in the second place I covered it. Of course, it could've gotten uncovered. Who knows? Besides, what was Chester Brown doing when he found it? Looking for it?

That Monday morning what Chester Brown had to say was: 'You said this job would be done in two weeks. This is the third week. Well?'

I told Tommy. And he said, "Well what?"

"Do you wanna answer it?" I asked.

"What's the point? If he wants the job done, it ain't done. But, if he wants us outta here, then I guess we're done. Does he tell us to leave?"

"No."

"Well then."

The reason it was taking longer was first the trouble with Rollie, and Tommy not having anyone to work with for a while. Then it rained so hard for a couple days we couldn't work. In fact about noon that Monday the sky opened up and we had to call it quits about one. At four I put on my rain gear and started for Monte Cassino. Beulah had been by. Checking up on me. Our notes were arranged like battalions on a field of war. Mine was surrounded by two of hers. Her latest one read: *Fence is out. Damn fool thing to do with moldy hay. Taking Jonathan home with me.*

Taking Jonathan home with her! So that's why he hadn't been with Felicia to greet me. I must just have missed them, the tide had only just gone out. I thought Felicia had seemed forlorn. Later I gave her extra hay; I know when I feel blue, eating's a comfort. The chickens, self-absorbed as a Girl Scout troop, didn't seem to care. But chickens don't give their softer emotions away. I'm sure they missed Jonathan; after all, they sleep on him.

I left this note: *Fixed the fence. I sunk a post where the wind keeps knocking it out. The chickens and Felicia are desolate. Too bad breaking up a happy home.* Then on second thought, I tore the last line off. It was about five o'clock by then and the temperature had dropped. I wondered whether it was going to snow. It does the end of June every so often, and the moon was full. It was really too cold and wet to sink a fence post, but where I'd already committed myself in writing, I didn't have much choice. Damn near froze to death. All I had on was a sweat shirt under my slicker. But I got the post in and the fence attached. Went to turn the power on and nothing happened. Damn fence was down somewhere else. I just knew Beulah Big Nose would be out writing notes first thing tomorrow morning. So I put my hands in my pockets and started making the circuit to find the down spot. I started counter-clockwise. If I'd gone the other way, I would've found it inside five minutes. As it was, it took three quarters of an hour.

A limb had fallen on the line, but the wire wasn't broken, just grounded. I pulled off the branch, a bit of spruce, and beat it out of there. Just in time. The tide already covered the spit. Ten minutes more and I'd've been there all night. I did take just a minute to duck into Santa Clara's and leave a new note, on a fresh piece of paper. I kept the first part same as before, including about Felicia and the hens being desolate. But I changed the last line to read: *Especially the hens miss Jonathan; they sleep with him.* I thought that was better, more subtle, less judgmental. I didn't want to be judgmental.

Next day, Tuesday, was wet and cold, but no downpour. I took care of the animals, giving Felicia a little extra hay to keep her busy and happy. No new notes, of course. Leaving, I noticed the van again and the guy at the wheel taking a nap. Odd once, weird twice. It's not like he could've been waiting for someone.

Except for me, coming from Monte Cassino, there wasn't a soul within a mile of there. It's all paper company land except for Newall's little apple orchard, but no one lives at Newall's. And there's no apples in June. I thought about going over and asking for a light. Just to get a closer look at him. But I would've had to ask him for a cigarette, too, and he might have thought that a little cheeky.

Tommy and I put in a decent day's work on Chester Brown's deck. "How much longer do you think?" I asked.

"Finish this week the weather holds," said he. I was hoping he'd tell me about another job he wanted me to help him with. But he didn't. It was easy, what with the wet and cold, to worry about the rent due Friday, and the money I owed Sopers. We worked along in silence until lunch which we ate in the cab of the truck. It was freezing cold. My fingers ached. I couldn't feel my toes at all. Tommy had hot soup in a thermos and he shared it with me.

"Rollie's getting out next week," he said in a brooding sort of way, not happy. Something funny happened to my heart.

"Oh yeah?" I said like everything was cool with me.

"Eyup."

"I thought he was in for a year."

"Is."

"Then how's he gettin' out? It's only been a month."

"Releasing him to Monte Cassino." Feeling the knife turn, I recognized the funny feeling in my heart as blood. Betrayed, and by that old do-gooder Lennie Soper.

"Lennie fixed it up?" My voice sounded strange to me, but Tommy didn't seem to notice. He just kept blowing on his soup.

He said, "Eyup."

After a while, after a couple sighs I couldn't suppress, I said, "Guess you won't be needing me any more."

"How's that?" he said. "Oh, you mean cause of Rollie getting out? Naw. He can't go off island except he's with one of them nuns."

"Oh yeah?" I said, feeling better. For a while. But we finished lunch and Tommy still hadn't said anything about my continuing to work with him. He seemed broody, and I was afraid to ask did he still want me as a partner?

When I drove down to the spit that evening, I found the dinghy was on the island shore, and I could see smoke. Benedict was back. I left without going across. At home I had a lonely meal of pizza from Pie in the Sky Pizza of Blue Hill.

Next morning I arrived too early and had to wait a while before I could cross over. The sky was leaden, low and heavy. You couldn't see Soper's Ridge at all and the firs along the shore looked bleak as the Berlin Wall. Checked Santa Clara's for notes. There were six of them. Two of Beulah's outflanked by three of mine. But a note by Sister Benedict was the leader of the pack. Her note read: *We need sawdust! Cleaned out the barn finally. What a mess!!! Cleaned chicken coop too. Boarded up a rat hole I found there.*

Rat hole! Asshole. That was the walk-through I made so the hens could visit Jonathan at night. I pointed all this out in my note, of course, and said I would get sawdust. I decided to ignore the imputation I hadn't kept the barn clean. After I fed Felicia and the hens, I unboarded the hole.

Right before I left I added a line to my note. Completed, it read: *Got sawdust for the barn. The hole in the chicken coop is so the chickens can have access to the barn on cold nights. Lennie says you should just add sawdust to the barn in winter and wait til spring to clean it out.* I had debated all the while I did the chores, should I say 'access to Jonathan', or 'access to the barn'. Access to Jonathan seemed too suggestive somehow, too access-to-Santa Clara-like, especially with

Sister Benedict around to read it.

It was going to be tricky getting the sawdust, getting it back to the island, not getting stuck for the day on Monte Cassino when the tide came in, getting to work on time. But where I'd written the note, it didn't seem I had much choice.

The van was there on the highway again, the fat head in the fedora pretending to be asleep again. I buzzed on out to Violette's, the lobster trap factory on Route 1, for sawdust. Was in such a hurry I only half fastened down the tarp and lost a good part of my load tearing down Route 15 there between Blue Hill and Monte Cassino.

Through the amber blizzard blowing in my wake, I thought I saw that van following me, and it sure wasn't parked on the shoulder by Newall's any more. The tide was lapping the surface of the spit as I drove across. Didn't I hurry! I would have swum back before I'd've spent a whole day on Monte Cassino with Benedict.

We all but finished the deck that day. Probably could've finished it if we'd tried. But it wasn't a day for extending yourself, temperature in the eighties, sun hot as a teen-age lover, bees in the lilac putting your brain to sleep with their buzzing. Black flies gorging themselves before their long goodbye. Black flies were all that kept us awake.

After lunch, Tommy said, "Could maybe give it two coats of polyurethane today. We'd be done." His head was shrouded in a fine mist of flies. You can tell a native, they don't seem to notice. "But tomorrow's just as good. Mayhap safer. Humidity," he added. He wiped some sweat from his brow with his thumb. "Eyup. Tomorrow." He still had said nothing about more work.

I asked, "Want me to leave C.P. a note? We'll be done tomorrow.?"

"Naw. Let him figure it out." He said, "Was hoping we could start on Drinkwater's barn tomorrow. You think you could finish up here on your own? Should only take 'n hour or two. You still got that truck?"

Cool wasn't in it. All I said was "Eyup," and kept on cleaning my brush. I said, "Want me over to Drinkwater's when I'm done here?"

"Eyup," said Tommy.

Eyup. I still had a job.

That evening, bored and lonely, I went out to Monte Cassino. Sister Benedict had spread the sawdust I'd dumped that morning. "Probably'll take credit for getting it too," I grumbled out loud to myself. Didn't see hide nor hair of her. No smoke either, of course, seeing how hot it was.

I checked Santa Clara's for notes, but there weren't any new ones. I knew Benedict had read mine, because she'd gone and boarded up the walk-through again. Guess the chickens having access to Jonathan on cold nights made her anxious. I knew how she felt. Myself, I couldn't keep my eyes off the door between Anne's so-called bedroom and Santa Clara's. Looking at it, I felt my brain burgeon with notes. This one I actually committed to paper: *I boarded up the rat hole between your room and the chicken coop, the one you and I put in two years ago. Forever yours, Alex.* Then I tore it up and put the pieces in my pocket. I decided before I did something irreparably stupid, I had better leave.

Trucking down Route 15 I saw them, Clara and Anne and about seven refugees, Indians, hair straight and dark, eyes dark. They were all laughing at something. I wished, savagely, I'd left one last note, like a time-bomb to go off in their faces, to eradicate their laughter. To blast from my mind that image of happiness passing by me. Passing me by.

Chester Brown's note that last day was brief: *Who's that bimbo you got working for you?* He had scrawled it across a sheet of foolscap. Underneath I printed, *Your deck's done.* And signed it *Bimbo.* The note was tacked to the back door, which is where he always leaves his notes. It only took an hour to finish with the polyurethane and for once I worked it so I ended up at the stairs, not in a corner. The only trouble was I'd thought up a better note to leave Mr. Chester Brown and there wasn't a thing I could do about it. And I sort of wished I had his note to show to Tommy.

I told Tommy about it as soon as I saw him. I said, "Where's that asshole from I wonder." Even though Tommy would never say ass-hole (he wouldn't say 'shit' if his mouth was full of it), I noticed his friends all did, so I took the liberty too. Also, it felt good to say shit and ass-hole and stuff after the long prohibition of Monte Cassino.

"Away," said Tommy laconically.

"Away!" I cried. "Away!" I must still have been hurting, seeing Clara and Anne and all those refugees laughing and having a good time together, carrying on like some big family, all intimate and happy. "Away isn't an address, you know,"I said. "I'm from away."

"Naw," said Tommy.

"Naw? Whadda ya mean naw?"

"Aren't you from Sullivan? Sorrento?"

I knew he was pulling my leg. Sullivan and Sorrento, they're a little further downeast, twenty miles maybe. But didn't I feel flattered he even said it, that I was from Maine, not from away.

We worked the rest of the afternoon in amicable silence. What Farmer Drinkwater wanted was a second story on his barn. It looked like I'd be busy most of the summer. I decided to get me a telephone. When the telephone came, three days later, the first person I called was Scott. We talked about this and that. He told me he was in love.

"So Anne didn't break your heart?" I said.

"Anne?" he said. Youth.

"Yeah. Anne. That bimbo you brought to Monte Cassino. The one who's living with Santa Clara. Remember?"

"Oh, Anne. You shouldn't call her a bimbo, Mom." He was right. I shouldn't.

I got to telling Scott about all the notes. Starting with that last one by Mr. Chester Brown calling me a bimbo. I told him about Benedict's note accusing me of not cleaning the barn.

I described how mad I got at Beulah's notes, and the note C.P. left about pooping in the woods. I got myself right worked up.

"Hey, take it easy, Mom," Scott suggested after a while. He said, "Let me give you some advice: In my experience someone leaves you a note, don't even look at it. And don't ever read one. Any note I ever read in my whole life it was bad news of one sort or another. Trust me, Mom. You're better off not to look at notes. Don't even think about reading them."

CHAPTER EIGHTEEN—LAVENDER'S GREEN

Dilly dilly.

Three days later, Anne got arrested. Spent the night in jail, too. Wasn't everyone upset! Beulah, Benedict, Agnes. And me. Santa Clara was frantic. Put up Monte Cassino as surety for bail, though I heard Sister Benedict threatened to throw the whole community out if Santa Clara went through with it. "Good God!" Sister Benedict is reported to have said, "Here is my mother supporting this community which you are jeopardizing the whole thing for those communists. From Honduras!"

Actually, they were from Guatemala. But I guess Benedict's family felt those distinctions didn't amount to a difference. My informant, via Tommy, was Rollie, who had moved to the community on Friday. Anne got arrested on Sunday for transporting that carload of refugees I saw. According to Rollie, Monte Cassino was like a beehive someone took a stick to, only most of the commotion was caused by the Queen Bee herself, Santa Clara.

The next day, Monday, the last day of June, Tommy and I began to raise the roof on Drinkwater's barn. The flies weren't too bad, too hot, besides they don't go indoors. The barn is situated on a knoll in Sedgewick overlooking Union Bay and all the islands. On a clear day, which it was that morning, you can see Isle Au Haut, whale-like and blue on the horizon.

In Maine, everything's some shade of blue. Even grass is more turquoise than green, except in the distance, then it's slate-colored. I would never have noticed, but Maria pointed it out to me up in Chesuncook that fall. Her painter's eye. But once you've seen it, everything being blue, then you're aware of it all the time. Straddling a beam in the afternoon, toenailing the first truss, seeing all that blue, the water, land, trees, grass and haze, all of it blue, I thought of Maria. And I kept right on thinking about her, so that in the evening when the phone rang and it was Maria on the line, I wasn't even surprised. It was like we'd just been talking, but in fact I hadn't heard from her in years. Until that afternoon, I hadn't thought about her either. Much. Santa Clara had, if nothing else, taken my mind off Maria. But hearing her husky voice, with that unidentifiable accent, I felt my heart do a funny two-step.

"You made the news," she said.

"I did?" I asked. "How's that?"

"Well. Your honey."

"I don't have a honey." My emotions, a witch's brew of precious bane and bats' blood, seethed. Lonely and longing, and resentful as hell, underneath it all I was afraid of getting involved again.

"You know," she said. "Clara."

"How'd you hear about it?"

"Danny. He saw it on the news. This woman getting arrested and she lived on Monte Cassino. Said he thought at first it was you."

"Naw. I don't live there any more."

"Oh."

"How'd you get my number?" I asked after a while. Just listening to her breathing like that, soft in my ear, her not talking, just breathing, in and out, made me nervous; in a minute I knew I would start to babble.

"Information," she said.

"Oh," I replied. Then I said, "Just got the phone. Just moved out—three weeks ago? Yeah, first of June. The lilac was in bloom. Got a lilac right outside my bedroom window, like I always wanted. Course, it's outside my kitchen and my living room window, too. Just have the one room. No Murphy bed, though." God knows when I would have stopped if Maria hadn't interrupted me.

"Who was the woman they arrested?" she asked.

"Oh, her. That was Anne. Umh, she and Santa Clara, they're an item."

"An item?"

"Yeah," I said. "Are you still with Maj?"

"Are you kidding? We split up years ago. You knew that."

Yeah, I did. But it was my heart asking, perverse thing; and what it wanted to know was: are you with anyone now?

"I'm not seeing anyone, actually," Maria said. "Hard to believe, isn't it. I guess I'm getting old. You're probably a grandmother."

"Actually, I am. Jennifer. She has a little girl."

"She married?"

"Yeah. You know Jennifer." Jennifer disapproved of irregular liaisons, beginning with mine and Maria's.

Then I got to describing my apartment, the view of the harbor, and the view from the ridge pole of Drinkwater's barn, of blue islands in a blue bay. I talked about light, light in haze, light in mist and fog, and the look of things when it was clear, each leaf and silhouette of pointed fir cut clean. It might have been Danny talking to her, and in the end she agreed to come and see for herself, to bring her easel and her paints, to stay, perhaps, a while.

The rest of that week all I heard about the goings-on at Monte Cassino I heard through Tommy. Tommy and Scott. Scott started calling me every morning about seven, before the rates go up. He seemed to regard himself as the impresario of a major production. He was in touch with the Center for Constitutional Rights in New York City, and with the AFSC Sanctuary Committee; he spent his days hanging out in the Cambridge Baptist Church making friends with everyone working on Central America. He thought Santa Clara should hold a press conference. "Get Sister Clara to hold a press conference, Mom. She should do that right away."

"She's not a Sister," I said.

"The longer she waits, the less public support she's gonna get. Has she spoken with the Bishop yet?" he asked.

In my mind I could see Santa Clara, her chainsaw spitting pink gobs of oil on the scarlet carpet of the Diocesan palace, and the Bishop cowering before her. "I don't think so, no."

"Well, she should do that right away."

"Scott, I never see the woman. You tell her."

That's approximately how the conversations went Monday, Tuesday and Wednesday mornings. Of course there were stories every day in the *Bangor Daily*. Monday, under the headline **Refugees Arrested in Calais**, there was an account of Anne's arrest for the crime of having brought the refugees back across the border.

Sanctuary worker Anne Gristead expressed surprise at the INS action. "Canadian immigration called the INS in Bangor," Ms. Gristead said, "to ask if they had a problem letting the family stay in this country while they waited for their hearing. INS said no problem. So I brought them back."

Ms. Gristead said the hearing in Canada was scheduled for July 14. When asked to verify Gristead's account of these events, INS officer Chester Brown flatly denied her story.

"It's none of it true," Brown maintained. "Canada never called our office. And if they had, we would have said no way. They can't enter this country. They're illegal aliens. All of them."

Canadian Immigration in St. Stephen's, however, backed up Gristead, saying they had placed a call to the INS office in Bangor. Canadian immigration officer Wade Tolliver expressed amazement at the border arrests.

The six Guatemalan refugees were released on their own recognizance Sunday evening. Ms. Gristead, however, was held overnight pending the posting of bail. The car used for transporting the subjects was impounded by the INS.

On Tuesday, the *Bangor Daily* reported that bail had been made and Anne Gristead had been released from custody. Her car, however, remained in the hands of the U.S. Immigration. Scott called me Tuesday night all excited.

"Mom! you gotta call that reporter from the *Bangor Daily*. He sounds sorta sympathetic. Ask him whether INS plans to take the family to Canada for their hearing."

I said okay I would.

Wednesday, sitting on the pole beam of Drinkwater's barn, surveying the universe and feeling like a queen, like I always do sitting on top of the world like that, I told Tommy about Scott's morning phone calls and about Scott's assigning me to call the *BDN*.

Tommy laughed. "No need to," he said.

"Oh yeah? Why's that?"

"They're lettin' Anne take 'em to Canada for their hearing."

"How can she? They impounded her car."

"Yeah but, they're lettin her drive them to St. Stephen's in it."

Sure enough, the paper next day quoted Immigration officer Chester Brown as saying, *The INS has made special arrangements for the family to be in Canada for their hearing on the 14th of July.* But he refused, the article said, to explain what the special arrangements were.

Scott told me Friday morning that the Center for Constitutional Rights had promised their best lawyer to fight the case for Anne.

During our mid-morning break from manhandling plywood boarding into place on the roof, I said to Tommy, "Scott's apparently got a good lawyer all lined up for Anne."

Tommy laughed. "No need to," he said.

"Whatta ya mean?"

"Rollie says what they need out to Monte Cassino's a lawyer, the way they're always arguin' about what lawyer to get."

"Oh yeah?"

"Sister Benedict, she says her mother's hired that Sullivan guy, you know, the one got Ollie North off? Well, as good as got him off. You ask me."

I nodded. "Yeah. Sullivan. She would."

"Well, Sister Clara says she wants someone else, I forget his name. Hustler? Somethin like that. He defended some black gal once, name of Angel, Rollie says."

"Angela Davis."

"That's right."

"Kuntsler."

"That's it. That's the guy."

Saturday morning I reported this to Scott when he called. "Sounds like they got enough lawyers already," I said.

"Too bad," said Scott. "Branigan's coming anyway. Now you tell Anne he's the one that she's to use."

"Yeah, I'll run right over and tell her," I said, but I don't think he even heard me.

He said, "Branigan's leaving for Maine today, should be there this evening."

I could have cared less. Maria, too, was scheduled to arrive that evening. She said to expect her for dinner. I begged off work a little early and hitched a ride into Blue Hill. I got some basil for pesto, and spinach linguini. Feta cheese and Greek olives for salad. Walked over to Pie in the Sky Pizza and asked if they would sell me a couple of crusty rolls; I told them it was for a very special occasion, and they did.

I told you Maria has red hair, too, didn't I? Well, she does. Her parents were from Donegal. Maria got more from her Irish background than red hair, however. She's always late for everything. When she finally got to Blue Hill, it was Saturday only in the sense that the sun hadn't risen; technically, it was Sunday morning. And I had fallen asleep at the kitchen table, the spaghetti water simmering slowly on the stove. I said, "Hello. I'm going to bed."

She said, "I thought we were going to have dinner. I'm starved."

Next morning I was up at four as usual. Another clear day. Standing at the window, I saw the rim of the universe etched in coral. I longed to show it to Maria. I longed to show her that fine line, so rosy with hope, cracking open the void, black and pregnant, bursting with an unseen day.

"Would you like to hang that on your wall?" she whispered in my ear.

Later on we had breakfast in bed.

CHAPTER NINETEEN—PURPLE

For all those things I'd rather see than be.

This one last chapter and then I'm checking out for the night. It's a little after nine. The wind's not howling any more. Now you know who the body on the couch belongs to. The only question that remains is how I got stuck with it out here on this god-forsaken island.

After breakfast, Maria wanted to visit Monte Cassino.

"Why?" I asked. It was about eight-thirty and we were lying in bed drinking coffee. Bustello. My favorite. Maria had brought it. You can't get it in Maine. She had made us an omelet for breakfast. Cheese omelet and home fries.

She said, "I don't know. See where you've been living. Do I need a reason?"

I said, "I don't go out there."

She said, "Why not?"

I said, "Do I need a reason ?" We laughed.

After a while Maria asked, "You still in love with her?"

I said, "Nah." I reached over and touched Maria's hair, glowing in the morning sun. It seemed on fire. Her eyes, shaped like diamonds, are blue, deep blue, like the bay on a summer day. "Nah," I said again.

"I want to meet her," said Maria.

"Why?" I asked, watching fire run through her hair.

"I don't know. I just do. That's all."

"Well," I said, "you'll have to go by yourself."

So we got up and dressed and went in search of the *Sunday Telegram*. The tide table showed she could go to Monte Cassino any time between ten and four.

"Don't go get stuck out there," I warned.

"Not to worry," she said and blew me a kiss.

I thought, as she disappeared down the road, that woman blows me a kiss and it blows me away. I tried not to worry about how I would manage to get over her a second time. As it turned out, she barely made it off the island. Water, she said, had already covered the spit when she drove back across.

When it got to be four-thirty and no Maria, I started pacing. First in the apartment and then out front, up and down the block. When she did arrive, who did she have in tow but Rollie. I had never met him. He's impressive: about six-foot-four and all muscle. "Can we use your telephone?" asked Maria after she had introduced us.

"Sure. Come on up," I said. "I'll make us coffee."

"Rollie wants to call his girl. No phone on the island," Maria explained. While the coffee brewed and Rollie phoned, Maria described how she had picked him up by Newalls Orchard. "He was going AWOL. I figured for the afternoon I could pass for a nun, Sister Benedict's Formation Director. How's that sound? You ask me, she could use one." Maybe so, but the thought of Maria as anyone's Formation Director was bizarre.

Rollie's phone call resembled a breathing exercise interspersed on occasion with reassurances like, "Yeah, honey, I'm still here," or "I love you too." So, while Maria and I overheard one whole hour of it, we never felt we were intruding.

Maria said, "He wants to spend the night with her."

"Is she a nun?" I asked.

"Why not? If I am."

"Hey," I said. "You're from away. I guarantee you, everyone in Blue Hill knows where Rollie is right this minute."

"Alex, that's ridiculous," said Maria.

"Ridiculous or not, it's true. And if you try to deliver Rollie to his girlfriend, he's gonna spend the night in Thomaston."

She said, "Hmmm."

"Where's the boat?" I asked. "Can he row across?"

"No. It's on the island." In the end what we did, but only because Maria insisted, was to fetch Cheryl and turn the apartment over to the two of them. "For a conjugal visit," Maria said to Rollie. "Until one o'clock. At one, it's back to Monte Cassino with you, or I will personally see to it you are turned into a pumpkin. Or worse."

Maria and I sneaked out the back and had a leisurely meal and some beer at Pie in the Sky Pizza. And that is the story of how Maria earned Rollie's undying devotion. He seemed to feel he owed me one too. For cooperating, I guess.

That's why I thought it might have been Rollie upstairs when I first got here. If it wasn't a squirrel. It's insane to think it might have been Clara. Whatever. It left. I'm not going to worry about it.

Over our second pitcher of beer, Maria started to talk about her visit with Santa Clara. "Poor Alex," is the way she began. I was feeling mellow. The beer, the pizza, the place. Pie in the Sky Pizza is out of the '60s. The women all wear long cotton skirts, the men all wear beards. The kids run around, unwashed and unsupervised, having a hell of a good time. The '6Os, that's when Maria and I were together before. Like I said, I felt mellow.

"Poor Alex?" I asked, kind of muzzy from the beer. "How come poor Alex?"

Maria said, "She really was a nun, hunh?"

"Santa Clara? Yeah."

"I hope there weren't too many like her in the convent."

"Yeah," I said. And then I said, "Why's that?"

"Poor Alex," said Maria again. After a while, Maria observed, "She's very seductive."

"Who?"

"Your honey. Clara."

"I don't have a honey," I said.

She said, "The hell you say! What about me?"

"Yeah," I said. "We're an item."

"An item! Where'd you pick that up?"

"Item? *People.* You know, the magazine."

"Since when," she said, "do you read *People*?"

"I don't," I said. "Too vulgar, calling people items. Stuff like that. Trash!"

She laughed.

"So you find Santa Clara seductive," I said.

"Not 'I find.' She is. She does. I walked in that door and the look she gave me. Whew!" Maria gestured putting out a match. "Don't tell me you never noticed?" she asked.

Noticed? Of course I'd noticed. Santa Clara looked at me that special way, and I would've walked off the Golden Gate Bridge for her if that's what she wanted. I used to think of it as catching a glimpse of eternity in her eyes. It had never occurred to me until just that moment, sitting in a pizza parlor drinking beer, that Santa Clara had ever in her life looked at another soul the way she used to look at me. Now here was Maria, a total stranger to Clara, describing my look as common property. Conjuring an image in my mind of little Santa Clara driving all the girls in the convent wild. Wild as she used to drive me. An image, suddenly, of Santa Clara turning Maria on. Of Maria being gone that afternoon for three hours, almost missing the tide even after I had warned her. Almost spending the night on Monte Cassino.

Stiffly, I said, "So she turns you on."

Maria laughed. "Oh, Alex," she said. "No. Or yes, I guess she does. But that's not why I stayed so long. How should I put it? I appreciate the technique. But I can't imagine falling for it." Not like dumb-ass here. "Also," she added. "Self-preservation. She's got that community by its collective tail. No pun intended."

Gloomily, I commented, "Yeah, it's called the Sister Benedict Syndrome." I told her about Beulah and Agnes and how Fr. Frank, observing the symptoms, had named the disease.

"I like that," said Maria. "The Sister Benedict Syndrome. Is it very painful?"

"Oh," I said. "There have been moments." I touched her hand. "But I've discovered this marvelous antidote."

"I bet you have," she said. "By the way, I think we could return Rollie to custody. Let me go call him and tell him we're on our way." When she got back, she said, "Incidentally, Rollie's got it bad, too."

"Got what bad?" I said.

"The Syndrome. Santa Clara says to Rollie 'jump!', he doesn't ask how high. He just starts jumping. With Rollie that could be dangerous." She said it pensively, as if in her mind's eye she could see the danger clearly.

By the fourteenth of July, the day of Anne's arraignment, Maria and I were broken in like an old pair of slippers. Not too romantic, but very comfortable. And comforting. On the wall above the bed, matted and framed, her new picture hung: A thin coral line cracking the void, a new day breaking.

The judge refused to commit Anne to trial. We were all surprised. Not that the INS had a case. Everyone in eastern Maine knew what fools they had made of themselves in the matter of the refugees who were trying to get out of the country. Chester Brown, who was frequently quoted in the *Bangor Daily News*, especially. But, it seemed to all of us, looking foolish hadn't stopped the government before, and none of us believed that looking foolish would stop them now. Judge Griswold, however, lost his patience when he heard how officer Chester Brown had let Anne take the refugees to their Canadian hearing in her impounded car. And he made a finding of 'insufficient cause' to put her on trial.

Chester Brown, of course, was at the hearing. That was

the first time I got a good look at him. And the last, alive. Turns out he was the same dude in the van and fedora who pretended to be asleep out by Newalls Orchard those mornings I took care of the animals at Monte Cassino. At the hearing, he sat up front behind the DA. He wore a chocolate brown polyester linen suit and yellow shoes. Not bright yellow, but yellow. Yellow like in yellow dog. You could see he was pissed at the verdict. He turned around and gave us a withering look, not that we were withered by it.

We were too elated. A bunch of us were sitting together on one of those long benches in the courtroom in Bangor. I was on the end. After the judge rendered his finding, Chester charged down the aisle. At our bench he paused and fixed his eye on me. He said, "Don't be too happy. You haven't heard the end of this. We still have RICO!" He jammed his fedora on his head, and started to leave. But before he went, he muttered under his breath, "And don't you ever lay your filthy red hands on my deck again."

After the hearing, the publicity died down real quick, but not the traffic in refugees; that picked up. They came pouring in from all over the country, especially toward the end of the year right before Canada's new, stiffer immigration law went into effect. By November, a family was coming through every five days or so. Scott brought many of them, so I saw him frequently. Maria offered to help with transportation on rainy days. She had begun to paint regularly, six days a week down on the dock. Except in downpours.

On several rainy days, and as the weather turned colder, she would drive to St. Stephen's with a carload. Everyone started learning Spanish. And going to church. All the refugees were devout. After the hearing and the scare, it all seemed like a lark, breaking the law and getting away with it. Like home fireworks on the Fourth of July. Illicit, but patriotic. Or, patriotic if illicit. Okay anyhow. And fun.

It wasn't until a little after Christmas that we heard from Chester Brown again. I'm still not sure that's his real name.

Maria had spent Saturday out to Monte Cassino. She and Anne had become good friends. She was, Maria said, sorry for Anne.

"Why's that?" I asked. This conversation happened on a lazy Sunday morning back in October. I know it was October, because we were lying in bed and I saw a leaf, all gold and red, like Maria's hair, fall against the window pane. It stuck there in the icy drizzle, so when the sun came shining through, the window looked like stained glass. Maria looked up at me scornfully, as though she couldn't believe I had asked her that.

"Well?" I said, puzzled. "Why are you sorry for Anne?"

Maria was lying with her head in my lap. She reached up and she touched my cheek. "Sister Benedict Syndrome? Ring a bell?"

Sister Benedict Syndrome! Three simple words, but didn't they leave me stunned. The dreadful thing is, my jealousy was aroused by the thought of Santa Clara being in lust again, and I wondered who it was. I said, "Oh."

"You don't need to worry," said Maria, as if to reassure me. I didn't get it until then.

"It's you!" I said.

"Yeah, but don't worry. Really"

Don't worry! I spent the afternoon tramping Blue Hill. So did lots of people. When I got back to the apartment, Maria said, "Trust me," which didn't help matters any. But during the next few weeks I came to believe that if Maria was going to get interested in someone else, it would be Anne, not Santa Clara. In any case, there wasn't anything I could do about it.

So, on this Saturday right before Christmas, Maria came back from Monte Cassino in a froth of indignation. "That ass-hole Chester Brown's at it again!" she said.

"At what again?" I asked.

"There's this grand jury and they're going to bring RICO indictments against everyone. And I'm really worried."

RICO, by the way, Racketeering and something or other, is federal legislation they passed ostensibly to make it easier to get convictions against people in organized crime. In practice, it's been used mostly to put political dissidents behind bars.

"That means me. And you too," Maria said.

"Why? I don't hang out at Monte Cassino."

"You don't need to. You're part of the conspiracy."

"What conspiracy?"

"The conspiracy to smuggle aliens out of the country."

"All I ever did was to pack you guys a lunch."

"That's enough. Anyway you did more than that." She started to laugh.

"Oh, yeah?" I said. "What's that?"

"You worked on Chester Brown's deck."

"Oh, right. And I pooped in his woods. Don't forget that."

"I won't. Neither will he. It should get you ten, maybe eight with good time. Aren't you glad you know someone at Windham? To show you the ropes?"

"Cut it out."

"I'm serious. But that's not what has me really worried." What had her really worried was something Santa Clara had said.

"If it weren't for Chester Brown," Santa Clara had announced before evening worship, "there wouldn't be any RICO charges." Then she said, "The only reason we keep on being harassed, is that Chester Brown."

"Well," I said, "that's so, isn't it?"

Maria looked exasperated. "You really don't understand, do you?"

"Understand what?" I asked.

"Think back," she instructed. "Think of all the things you used to do just because you thought that Clara wanted it."

I thought about it. She was right, of course. I remembered the conversations I used to conduct for the two of us, Santa Clara and me, always more careful to represent her fairly than myself. I'd told Maria stories about it and learned to laugh at them, a little. "Yeah," I said after a while. "So?"

"Remember," Maria said, "I told you she says to Rollie, jump, and he doesn't ask how high because he's already jumping, knowing he can jump higher than anyone else."

I nodded. I said, "You afraid he'll do in Chester Brown?"

She said, "Yes. I am." I didn't say anything. At the time I thought her fears were exaggerated. But the idea stuck in the back of my mind.

How I heard about the raid was on the Police scanner. That was two days ago. I've been here at Monte Cassino in this blizzard-without-end almost forty-eight hours. Maria had gone out to Monte Cassino, she said to help Anne put some bookshelves up.

When she told me, in the morning, I said, "Where? There's no room for more bookshelves in Santa Clara's bedroom." I thought Maria looked at me kind of funny. "Well," I said, "there isn't."

"Maybe not," said Maria. "I wouldn't know. Anne needs them in her room. She doesn't have a bureau or anything."

I mulled it over for a while. Until I thought I had it right. "Santa Clara kicked her out," I said.

"Yeah. You wanna move back in?"

"No. And you better not either." We laughed and it felt good.

I spent Monday reading Mary Webb's *Precious Bane*. My friend Erika Duncan, who gave it to me, wrote the introduction. She explains why it's one of her favorite books even though it is no longer fashionable to find its brand of sentiment appealing. Steadfastness and loyalty aren't supposed to be rewarded in these days of the anti-hero. Perhaps if I had been lost in a bit of magic realism, Marquez or Allende, not Mary Webb, I would have stayed at home and been content to listen to my scanner. Been content to imagine happy endings. But no. I had to run out in the storm and try to rescue people.

Along about six, it was dark already, I started to fix supper, expecting Maria home any time. The tide had turned. For company, I put the scanner on. I'd bought it with my second pay check. This is what I heard: "... static... back- up needed Route 15. Newalls Orchard. Can you take it, Tim?"

"... static...What's the problem?"

"Dunno for sure. Gotta call from Chester Brown. Something about immigration...static... Out to that Island they call Monte Cassino."

"Oh Lordy!"

"You said it!"

I was out of the house and on the road without ever having decided to. I just did it. I don't know who I intended to rescue. Or how I was going to get there. Walk I guess; it's about five miles. It had already started to snow. That didn't worry me. I knew they'd predicted flurries.

Out by Largay's a little old lady—she was about my age—stopped and picked me up. "Where you goin' on a night like this?" she asked.

"Down by Newalls Orchard," I said.

"You ain't one of them refugees?" she asked.

"Naw."

"Well," she said, "you be careful down there. They're having a raid. If the communists don't get you, the Immigration will. Heard it on the scanner."

It was pitch black when she dropped me off and snowing to beat the band. "Ain't you got no flashlight?" she asked as I hopped out.

"Nope."

"Well, you take this one," she said, picking up a big red flashlight lying on the seat beside her.

"I can't take that," I said.

She tossed it at me. "Return it to Largay's. Shut the door. And don't go getting your feet all wet. You'll catch your death a cold."

There was no one around. The tide was in, but I crossed

on the ice. Thanks to the flashlight, I managed to stay dry. No lights on in any of the buildings. No one seemed to be there. Just Jonathan and Felicia and the hens, the hens all huddled along Jonathan's back. I checked the barn, Santa Clara's room and Anne's. There were new shelves in the old chicken coop. I was surprised to see the hammer and drill lying on the floor. It looked like Maria and Anne had left in a hurry. I checked out Trinity and the retreat houses. Only one building left, Sister Benedict's down the hill. That's where I found Chester Brown. Dead. At the bottom of the stairs. By the time I found him it was snowing so hard I knew I couldn't get off the island, not in one piece. I didn't think I could even get back up the hill. So I stayed here. With him. Now you know the whole story. And I am going to bed.

Chapter Twenty – Pencil Stub

Just a note before I leave this place. It's a brilliant day, the sun making up for those two days it spent away, and getting all kinds of help from the snow. Hurts your eyes just looking where to put your feet. I really must have passed out when I finally went to bed last night. I decided I might as well go upstairs, sleep in Benedict's bed. Since the couch was occupied. No sign of anyone up there. The bed was unmade, but then I wouldn't have expected Benedict to make it. It smelled a little of diesel, but Benedict drives the truck, too. Anyway, I think I was asleep before my head hit the pillow. At one point, I seemed to be having a nightmare, a confused impression of someone breaking in downstairs. I'd think that I had gone to check it out, and then realize I'd only gone back to sleep and dreamed I'd checked it out.

Anyway, this morning I woke with the sun in my eyes. Couldn't think for a moment what it was! I staggered down the ladder, put wood in the stove, made coffee, then I was sitting there taking in the scene, everything so dazzling, blue glints like diamond chips sparkling on the snow, and I realized the body's gone. I looked out the door and you could see where a sled carrying a heavy load had been dragged away. Snow-shoe prints, or whatever, had been obliterated. Now what do you think about that?

Chapter Twenty-One – Pen

On yellow foolscap.

It took me forever to get off Monte Cassino. Climbing the hill was especially challenging, snow to my groin. Halfway up, I saw where the sled had veered off toward the cedar bog. Needless to say, I did not follow it. Whoever dragged that sled was some strong, let me tell you. And only one person I can think of is as strong as that. I made it across the spit before the tide came in, must have been close on noon. Weren't many cars out, but Route 15 was fairly clear, considering.

The first car picked me up; the driver was Mr. Jardins. He owns the pharmacy in town. "Some storm," he said. "For flurries."

"Yeah. How bout that!"

"What you doin" out this way?"

I lied reflexively. "Worried about the folks out to the island," I said.

"They okay?"

"Beats me. No sign of 'em."

"Probably got off before the storm hit. Sensible thing to do."

"Yeah. If they knew it was coming."

"Well, that's true. But ain't it always the ones they don't predict turn out the worst?"

"You're right there," I agreed, wondering, as usual, about

174

Jardin's Downeast, just-one-of-the-folks, twang. One of my fishing friends told me he'd come to Maine from Panama.

The apartment, when I got there, was a three-ring circus. A refugee family with two kids, a girl about four and a little boy about six, were there with Maria. The children were playing house, I guess. They had all the pots and pans on the floor and they were trying to construct a tent with blankets from the bed. The parents and Maria were sitting at the table drinking coffee. Maria, I thought, looked haggard, but everyone seemed cheerful enough.

"Thank god you had the brains to get a gas stove," Maria greeted me. "Or we would have frozen to death. The electricity's been out since sometime Friday night. Where've you been?"

"Me? Out on the island."

"This whole time?" I nodded. I nodded at Maria. Then I nodded at our guests. I found it hard to stop nodding. I felt light-headed and without volition. Whatever I found myself doing, nodding for instance, I kept right on doing. How I finally stopped my head from nodding is I caught hold of it with both my hands and held tight.

The refugees looked Mayan, black straight hair, broad cheekbones, delicate features. They were rolly-polly with layers and layers of clothing; I recognized shirts and sweaters of mine among them. The children approached, curious but wary, and stood behind their mother's chair, looking me over.

"Buenos dias," I said. "Buenos dias. Buenos dias." I let go of my head. It started to nod again.

They nodded. They said, "Buenos dias. Buenos dias." They seemed amused, a new gringo custom. "Buenos dias."

We said 'Buenos dias,' a few more times.

The children started to giggle. They said, "Buenos dias! Buenos dias!" but loud.

Maria broke it up. She said, "Alex, you look exhausted. Sit down. Let me get you a cup of coffee." I caught hold of my head again and followed her advice. Cards and little piles of matchsticks lay on the table. They had been playing poker. Maria said, "You don't have any food on you, by any chance. No? I didn't think so. We're out of everything but mold. We're saving that."

The coffee helped, and just having people around. Jaime, Elena and Maria went on with their poker game. The children went on looking at me from behind their mother's chair. After a while I suggested going to Largay's for food. It seemed to be what Maria was waiting for.

"Let's go!" she said. "I'm ready."

It took a while to unbury the car. Sitting in it, waiting for the engine to warm, Maria turned to me and said, "Alex, were you really at Monte Cassino this whole time?" I felt my eyes begin to sting with tears. "Careful," Maria said. "Don't cry. Your eyes'll freeze shut. Then I'll have to drive. You don't want me to drive. Not in this."

I started to laugh, but the tears kept coming. I said, "I love you."

"Glad to hear it," she said. She said, "Want to tell me about it?"

What I wanted was a nice hot bath, scented bath oil, a cup of tea, and Maria to scrub my back for me. Maria said, "There's no hot water, but when we get back, I'll heat some on the stove for you. And make you a nice cup of tea."

I said, "Won't you scrub my back?"

She said, "Of course I'll scrub your back."

I said, "We're out of bath oil."

"So?" she said. "They sell bath oil at Largay's. I'll get you some. What else do you want?"

What I wanted was to obliterate the weekend. Lose the image of Chester Brown's body lying at the foot of the ladder. Get rid of this feeling of evil that lay on my body like scum on a pond. I'd felt it ever since this morning when I discovered his body was gone. Ever since I had to stop kidding myself. I hadn't been alone out there. Someone else had been on the island with us. How close had I come to sharing Chester Brown's fate? To lie beside him in death. To sink with him, come spring, into the bog to feed the little sundews and the other carnivorous plants that flourished there.

"Oh, Maria! It was awful. He was dead, and I thought we were alone, and that was bad enough, but we weren't. Someone was there. They took his body away."

"Alex, shhh. Take it easy," she said. "Whose body?" She held me while I told her. Held me right there on Main Street, Blue Hill, Maine. It didn't incite a riot. People were too busy digging out from the snow. She interrupted me once in a while. Like when I told her I'd put Chester Brown's body on the couch and wrapped it in a quilt. "Why did you do that?"

"So he'd be comfortable. Oh, don't ask me. So I couldn't see him."

"I see," she said. And later: "Why didn't you look in the loft if you thought someone was up there?"

"What! Get myself killed? Besides, the noises stopped. I decided I must have been imagining things."

"Have you told the police?"

"How could I? Carrier pigeon? Smoke signals?"

"Don't be cross," she said. "I meant did you tell them today?"

Tears tasted salty in my mouth and I needed to blow my nose. Maria handed me a tissue. She stroked my cheek.

I said, "I can't go to the police. The body's gone."

"The body's gone?"

"That's right. Gone," I said. "Like bye-bye."

"Gone. Like the other person who was there?"

I said, "You don't believe me!"

She said, "Honey, of course I believe you. Let's get the bath oil and I'll put you in a nice hot tub."

"Don't you patronize me!" I said.

She started to massage my neck. "Your neck is all tense. It's hard as a rock."

I said, "I think Rollie took the body away."

She massaged a while. "You didn't see Chester Brown's car anywhere?"

"Well, I wouldn't have noticed. It was dark when I went over. It wasn't there this morning."

All she said was, "I see."

I would have gotten mad—I was mad—but I didn't want her to stop massaging my neck. "What I think is Rollie was out there. Who else could have lugged the body away. He could have taken the car, too."

She stopped massaging.

"Don't stop," I said.

She said in a tentative voice, or perhaps she meant it to be soothing, "You think Rollie killed Chester Brown?"

"Well, if I remember correctly, wasn't it you who said you were worried Rollie might do just that? Don't stop. If he thought that's what Clara wanted? Well?"

Maria didn't say anything, and though she continued her massage, it had become perfunctory.

After a while, I said, "At first I thought he must have fallen down those godamned stairs. I told Santa Clara a million times some day someone's going to break their neck on those stairs, and now they have. That's what I thought. But, Maria, please believe me, someone took the body away and the only person who could have is Rollie. I know you like him. I'm sorry."

"Alex," she said, "I do believe you. I believe there was a body and I believe Rollie must have been the one who took it away. "What I'm not so sure about is that he's the one who put it there."

Chapter Twenty-Two

After Maria had thoroughly scrubbed my back, she left me to soak. A drowsy half-hour. I heard the door bell ring and then a bustle of activity. After that quiet folded over the apartment like a down comforter. When I finally emerged, my skin all puckery from the tub, our company was gone. The apartment was picked up. And the bed, with fresh linen, was turned down. Maria sat in our one chair reading. She wears glasses when she reads, those little granny glasses with only half a lens. She looked at me over the top of them. "Feel better?" she asked.

"You bet. You comin to bed with me?"

"I thought you'd never ask," she said. A little later she told me about the goings-on at Monte Cassino before the storm broke. "Along about five in the afternoon—Anne and I had just about finished with the bookshelves—Lennie Soper drives up. He hems and haws, you know how he does, and finally he asks for Santa Clara, and when he's got us all together, he tells us he's just heard there's going to be this INS raid and they're looking to get evidence for the Grand Jury and put us all up on RICO charges. And he asks do we have any refugees there with us now.

"Then he covers his ears like this and he says, 'No, don't tell me. I don't want to know. Only, if you do, get 'em outta here PDQ. And,' he says, 'I mean any trace of them too.' With that he ups and leaves.

"Well, what to do? Anne and I, we volunteered to take the refugees and hide them.

"By this time, the storm's beginning to look serious and Benedict's hollering about how she told us this would happen and her mother's gonna kill her. She says she's washing her hands of the whole rotten business, and that means you, too, Clara, she says. Etc., etc.. And she's leaving. So's Agnes. Somehow we managed to get everyone off the island and I dropped the three of them—Agnes, Benedict and Anne—at the motel in town."

"A congenial group," I observed. "What'd you do with Clara?"

"She and Rollie were going to give the horses extra hay and come right along. They knew they didn't have much time, between the storm and the tide."

"Oh," I said. It must have sounded glum.

Maria said, "You're right. I didn't actually see either of them leave the island." After Maria had dropped the odd trio off at the motel, she brought the Guatemalan family home. "No one was here. The lights were on, the door unlocked. But no Alex. I missed you."

"That's nice," I said. "What about the INS?" I asked. "Did they ever do their thing?"

"Raid? I don't know. They didn't show up before I left. Obviously. Could they have come and gone before you got there?"

I said, "I don't see how. I couldn't have missed you by more than fifteen minutes...Oh my God!" I said.

"What's wrong?"

"I forgot that nice old lady's flashlight!"

"Scare me half to death!" Maria exclaimed. "I thought you told me she was your age. We'll take care of the flashlight tomorrow. Now, I think it's time we went to sleep."

Next day we got a few answers to our questions. Lennie Soper stopped by in the morning to see how we were. He said the INS raid never happened. "Nope," he said. "Got down to the spit there and it's already under a inch of water and the snow coming down. Some flurries! We none of us reckoned to spend the night on Monte Cassino. So we left. Never did go over."

"You mean," I said, incredulous, "Chester Brown just let you guys go home?"

"Funny thing," said Lennie, "he never showed."

"He didn't make it to his own raid?" Maria asked.

"Eyup. How about that. Less he was already on the island. Might've driven over, before we got there, I guess. His car wasn't nowhere. Haven't heard from him."

"That's funny," said I.

"Yeah," said Lennie. "I think so."

Next morning, there's a front page story in the *Bangor Daily* about a missing INS officer. One Chester Brown, aka Carlos Pardo. They never came right out and said it, but you could read between the lines what they were driving at was big time drug dealing. Big time. They said he was born in Medellin, so that right there told you what they were meant to imply. Anyway, they said he was missing and that the FBI had been called in to investigate. I asked Maria what she thought I should do about it.

"Well," she said, "first you better find out what Clara and Rollie know."

"Easier said than done," I said. "You know Clara. She'll just dummy up. Or," I said thoughtfully, "meditate at me."

"Well!" said Maria indignantly, "she just can't do that. Not about this. It's too important."

I wasn't so sure. That evening Anne came over. She had Rollie in tow. Maria questioned and then cross-examined him. He never wavered in his story which encompassed two simple points: He had left Clara on the island to weather the storm alone; and he had walked to Cheryl's where he stayed until Anne picked him up on Monday.

Maria said, "Weren't you afraid of being arrested?"

He said, "In a storm like that? You kidding? No way!"

Maria said, "How'd Anne know to pick you up?"

"Aw," said Rollie, "she's not as dumb as she looks. Only kidding."

"I think," pressed Maria, "you returned to the island early Sunday morning, to check up on Clara. And other things." She paused. "Like dispose of his car?"

Rollie didn't even blink when Maria mentioned the car. And no matter how she put her questions and veiled accusations to him, all Rollie ever said was, "No way."

After they left, Maria and I puzzled it out together. We agreed Rollie was lying about not having gone back to Monte Cassino Sunday morning. And we agreed he probably spent most of the storm at Cheryl's. As for the car, we figured it was probably already repainted and resold. Maria asked me for the umpteenth time, "You're absolutely positive Santa Clara wasn't on the island when you got there?"

"Yes. I'm absolutely positive. Santa Clara was not on the island. All the buildings were empty." Then I had a disquieting thought. "Was Clara coming down with a cold?"

"Why do you ask?"

"Whatever or whoever it was upstairs had some respiratory problem. And it sneezed some." Then I said, "That's a ridiculous idea, of course."

"What's ridiculous about it?"

"It just is. Obviously. Clara wouldn't do that to me." Even I could tell I was whistling in the dark.

Maria, kindly, said nothing for a while. Then she said, gently, "If you didn't see her, maybe she didn't know you were there."

"Right. And then what? She left by way of the window so she wouldn't disturb me while I was writing? Oh, I forgot! She's not supposed to know I was there. Come on, Maria!"

"Maybe she didn't want to see the body, maybe she figured she couldn't get out the door, the snow was too high."

"Good try," I said. Then, stubbornly, "It wasn't Clara.

Whoever it was had to know I was there. Clara wouldn't have left me alone all by myself in that storm with that dead body. Can we end this discussion now?"

"Honey," Maria's voice was gentle. "We're going to have to go find out, you know."

I said, "I hope that's a royal we."

"No, actually, it was a royal you."

"Oh, no," I said. "No way."

But go I did. Next morning. It was about ten o'clock. Had to wait at the spit before I could cross over. Once I'd made up my mind to go, I wanted to get it over with, didn't even check the tides. Across the way stood a funny little car, a kind of mongrel car, different colored doors, beside it a lady even more impatient than me. She was swinging her arms around and blowing on her hands. Musta been low on gas.

I'd brought a flask, Maria had given it to me at the door. I took a nip and then for a joke I put my head out the window and showed it to her nibs. "Want some?" I shouted. She must have had a hair across her butt, she didn't say a word, just got in her car and started the engine. I let her come across first.

Found out later her name's Brigid Donovan and she's in AA. How was I supposed to know?

Once across, I followed the sound of the chainsaw up Soper Ridge to Clara. "Hello, Alex," she said. She kept squeezing the trigger of her saw. Little red globs of sawdust and oil, like thick drops of blood, spattered on the clean white snow. It was hard to hear her above the angry buzz, like bees disturbed. Killer bees, I thought.

"Turn off that damn saw," I said.

She just kind of smiled. Her bandanna had slipped and a hank of brick red hair lay across her cheek. I once thought she looked vulnerable with her bandanna awry like that and her hair showing. Vulnerable and exposed. I searched her eyes for that once familiar hint of eternity I used to think I could see there. But her eyes seemed shallow. They seemed pale. In the dazzling light reflected from the snow, they seemed yellow. Giddy, I was reminded of Chester Brown's shoes. I shouted, "Where were you last weekend?"

"Here," she said. I couldn't hear her, just see her lips move.

"You weren't. I checked all the buildings. No one was here."

She shrugged. Twice her finger pressed the trigger of the saw. It screamed. A shower of red splashed the snow.

"What happened last Friday when Chester Brown showed up?" I yelled.

She shook her head. "He wasn't here," her lips said.

"Clara, it's no use. I was here. I know. Chester Brown died here last Friday night. Broke his neck on that ladder in Immaculate Conception. Rollie buried him in the cedar swamp as soon as the storm ended."

The saw stuttered and died. "If," said Santa Clara in her soft, controlled voice, "if you know all this, Alex, you must have been the last person to see him alive. It sounds to me like you could be in a lot of trouble. If people knew."

It may have been a trick of the light, but the irises of her eyes seemed to open and close, a kind of peristalsis of the soul. Then she said, "Don't mess with this, Alex. Just let it alone." I felt tears sting my eyes. "I think you should go," she said. "Rollie and I have a lot of work to do. We're building a shelter for homeless people and refugees. We want to have it finished by Easter. It's hard when people are cold and hungry and you have to keep dealing with constant interruptions."

As I made my way down the hill, I heard the crash of another tree.

Epilogue

Hasta Luego, Arizona

A year later. A little wiser. No richer. Maria created a wonderful series of paintings of villages along the coast of Maine. Blue Hill especially. She had a show that summer in Rockport. And later, one in Manhattan. Uptown!

Anne moved back to Texas around the first of February. She and Scott are still good friends. So are she and Maria. I don't think she and I will ever be good friends. That Sister Benedict Syndrome is a little like malaria. You might get over it, but it stays in your blood.

Benedict, Agnes, Santa Clara and Rollie are still at Monte Cassino, plus, at any given time, a dozen or so homeless people, and/or refugees. Chester Brown's there too, I guess. In the cedar bog. He was never found. And I never said anything.

That winter the news of Winnie Mandela's Football Club broke and everyone was saying how they just couldn't believe it. I could believe it. And I thought I could understand it. I could understand the Football Club, and even Jonestown. It has to do with power, especially the kind of power a charismatic personality commands. It's true, power corrupts. What Lord Acton didn't mention is that there are different kinds of power. Winnie Mandela's power, like Jim Jones's, like Santa Clara's, was power over other people's will.

Power of this sort results in behavior that seems inconceivable. Much is said about the eyes of charismatic leaders. But the power is also in their message, that promise of being part of an inner circle, one of the Chosen Few. Their victims, if that's what you want to call them, are willing. More than willing. I know.

Well, that's my cosmic explanation. I tried it out on Maria and her comment was: "Oh, Alex, there you go again!" I must have looked miffed. She said, "It's nothing but control. Why men beat up women, police beat on Blacks. Some people need to control other people. Give them the power, that's what they're gonna do. It's got nothing to do with their eyes. I'm sorry."

She explained later that I had made her miss a unique effect of sunset on the desert, something about moisture. I didn't get it. Personally, I think Maria and Acton didn't get it either.

I'm not in Maine anymore. I'm on a fat farm in Arizona. A cook, not a client. Maria and I were sitting around after work one evening in September and Maria says, all bright and eager, "I got a letter from Jim-Jim today."

"Okay," says I, "I'll bite. Who's Jim-Jim?"

"Honey! Didn't I ever tell you about Jim-Jim?"

"No, dear heart. You never told me about Jim-Jim. Do I want to know?"

"Oh, certainly. Jim-Jim was my very first husband. We were sixteen. High school sweethearts."

"Oh oh!"

"No 'oh oh' about it. Trust me. He's got this fat farm in Arizona. Wants to know would we like to come cook for him this winter. He says the winter light in the desert has to be seen to be believed." Maria seemed to believe it. I did too. It's been fun.

THE KALI CONNECTION A Lynn Evans Mystery by Claudia McKay
Lynn, an investigative reporter is checking on the connection of a mys-
terious Eastern cult with possible drug trafficking. Her attraction to
Marta, a charming and earnest devotee challenges Lynn's skepticism
and sparks her desire. Then Marta disappears. Lynn travels to Nepal
to find some answers. $9.95

DEATHS OF JOCASTA   by J.M. Redmann
Micky's lover, Dr Cordelia James is accused of murdering her patients.
How can Micky prove her innocence? "Knight is witty, irreverent and
very sexy." $10.95

DEATH BY THE RIVERSIDE   by J.M. Redmann
Detective Micky Knight, hired to take a few pictures, finds herself slug-
ging through thugs and slogging through swamps in an attempt to
expose a dangerous drug ring.   Featuring fabulously sexual, all too
fiercely independent lady dick. $9.95

FIGHTING FOR AIR   A Cal Meredith Mystery by Marsha Mildon
Jay's class of scuba students goes out for their first open water dive.
One of them comes up dead. And it turns out lots of people had good
reasons to kill him. $10.95

IF LOOKS COULD KILL   by Frances Lucas
Diana Mendoza, a Latina lesbian lawyer is a scriptwriter for a hot new
TV show featuring a woman detective. While on location in LA she
meets blonde actress Lauren Lytch. When Lauren is accused of murdering her husband, Diana rushes to her defense. $9.95

SOME ALISON KAINE MYSTERIES by KATE ALLEN

TELL ME WHAT YOU LIKE
Alison Kaine, lesbian cop, enters the world of leather-dykes after a
woman is brutally murdered at a Denver bar. She's fascinated, yet
wary of her attraction to one of the suspects, a dominatrix named
Stacy. In this fast-paced, yet slyly humorous novel, Allen confronts the
sensitive issues of S & M, queer-bashers and women-identified sex
workers. $9.95

GIVE MY SECRETS BACK
A well-known author of steamy lesbian romances has just moved back
to Denver when she is found dead in her bathtub. Suspecting foul
play, cop Alison Kaine begins an off-duty investigation to find the
chapters of her next book which are inexplicably missing, and may
contain clues to her murder. $9.95

I KNEW YOU'D CALL   A Marta Goicochea Mystery
Phone psychic Marta and her outrageous butch cousin Mary Clare try
to help a friend accused of murder. "It grabbed me from the first page
and wouldn't let me go...a gritty, impressively real and thought-pro-
voking lesbian mystery." Ellen Hart $10.95